2nd book in "The Journal Series"

The Cowboy of Her Dreams

By

Stephanie Payne Hurt

The Cowboy of
Her Dreams
The Journal
Stephanie
Payne Hurt

Stephanie writes a variety of books ranging from Christian romance to sweet romance to historical romance. This list is as of April 20, 2020, but there are many more to come soon! Check out my website for all the newest cover reveals of upcoming books!

Stand Alone
Falling Snow
Finding the Right Time
Holly Cottage
Mountain Bliss
Seaside Beginnings
The Christmas Wish
Tuscany
You Were My World
To Dance with Dragonflies

5 Oaks Ranch Series
Ridge
Oakley
Chase
Luke
Maggie
A Christmas to Remember

Alpine Romance Series
Open the Heart
Lacey's Choice

And the Winner is Love Series
The Winner is Love
The Winner Takes All

Fall in Love with a Cowboy Collection
A Love Never Lost
Ghost Lover
Moonbeam & Roses

Fall in Love at Sea Collection
Safe in the Pirate's Arms
The First Mate's Lady

Flames of Love Collection
Tender Flames
Rekindled Flame

Cowen Clan Series
The Highlander's Heart
The Highlander's Bride
The Highlander's Son

Lean on Him Collection
With All My Heart
Faith Through the Tears
Her Wish for Christmas
Sowing the Right Seed

Woman of Magnolia Hill Saga
Victoria
Emma Rose
Lily
Georgia

Mail Order Bride Collection
A Light Upon my Heart
When Spring Comes

Mistletoe Ranch Series
Christmas at Mistletoe Ranch
Wedding at Mistletoe Ranch – Coming
Soon!
Double Take at Mistletoe Ranch – Coming
Soon!

Sky Ridge Series
Promises Made
Promises Forgotten
Promises Kept

The Journal Series
The Knight of her Heart
The Cowboy of her Dreams
The Pirate of her Desire – Coming Soon!
Marina's Story – Coming Soon!

Tangled Vines Collection
Beyond One Moment
Tarnished Silver

Wishful Harbor Collection
Breakwater Lane
Hideaway Lane
Inlet Circle
Pier Cove – Coming Soon!
Bay Street – Coming Soon!

Budget Book – Nonfiction

Chapter 1

Rain had to come to grips with her sister's disappearance, but she understood that love could make you do crazy things and Rain wanted what Willa had found. She knew the way to her dreams was through her ancestor's journal.

She grabbed her favorite pen and picked up the journal, opening it to the first yellowed page. The editor in her stared at the blank page, unsure of where to start, then something inside of her heart began to flow through her. The words poured out on the page and before she knew what was happening, she was slipping into darkness.

The moment she opened her eyes, Rain was confused. Where was she? Then she was thrown forward into the floor of what looked to be a stagecoach. The world outside was racing by the windows as the stagecoach flew across the uneven road. Rain struggled to get back up.

Just as she got a grip on the side of the seat, a voice from outside the stagecoach yelled. Rain looked out of the window and only a few feet away from the runaway stagecoach, a cowboy was keeping up with her. He was pointing straight ahead and motioning for her to look.

Rain leaned her head out the window to see what he was trying to show her. A screech ripped from her throat as she saw the wide ravine not far ahead of them.

She looked back at the cowboy, fear taking over. Surely, she hadn't been sent back in time to die within minutes of arriving. Rain sat back and thought of all the westerns she'd read, trying to remember how damsels escaped runaway stagecoaches; but nothing was coming through her head.

A sound beside Rain made her jump. The cowboy was clinging to the side of the coach.

"Hold on ma'am." He yelled in the window, then proceeded to climb up onto the seat of the coach.

Rain couldn't respond as she watched him from the window. After several shouts to the horses, the stage came to a rocking halt.

"Ma'am are you alright?" The cowboy said as he snatched the door open.

Rain looked at him, pinching herself because she just knew this couldn't be happening. "You can't be real." She rasped out as dust billowed around inside the stagecoach. A cowboy had just saved her from a runaway stagecoach. This was like something out of one of her dreams.

"Did you hit your head?" Sloan said, a grin on his handsome face.

"No, I don't think so." Rain managed to say. The man standing beside the coach was nothing short of amazing. He was taller than any man she'd ever seen and the way his cowboy hat shaded his eyes made him look mysterious.

"Here, take my hand and I'll help you out." Sloan held out his hand. At first, she didn't take it, but only stared at it.

"Ok, thanks." Rain said, then she slid her small hand into his large work roughened hand. Their eyes met as something passed between them, but the feeling went away as quick as it came.

"Ma'am, I don't have all day." Sloan said as his eyes roamed over her strangely clothed body. Why was this woman wearing men's trousers?

"I'm sorry. But it wasn't you in this runaway stagecoach, about to plummet to your death, was it?" Rain snapped, sparks of anger flying as she pushed his hand aside and climbed out on her own.

"Look lady, the driver will be here in a moment, so you can continue on your way." Sloan turned, needing to get his eyes off the woman he'd rescued. She was a tiny wisp of a thing with auburn hair and huge green eyes. She had a tongue like a viper, and he didn't need that in his life right now.

"Where was this stage headed?" Rain asked as she looked around, trying to figure out where she'd ended up.

Sloan swung around with a strange look on his face. "Excuse me. Did you just ask where the stage was headed? Didn't you know when you booked passage on it?" Sloan looked up to the baggage rack and saw there was nothing there. "Where's your baggage?"

Rain shrugged, "I don't have any baggage and no, I didn't know where it was headed. When I opened my eyes, I was already on the stage."

Sloan reached up and pushed his hat up on his forehead to get a better look at her. "Did you just say that when you woke up, that's where you were? Were you kidnapped?"

"Not that I know of." Rain said with a frown. She'd best stop talking like a crazy person or this man would have her thrown into an insane asylum. "I mean, well, I must have forgot where I was going."

"Where is that driver at?" Sloan looked back toward where the stage came from. He had to get back to his ranch and away from this sharp-tongued woman that looked like an angel in men's clothing. There was one thing he knew and that was he didn't need to be drawn into this woman's drama.

"I think I'm lost." This wasn't happening the way Rain had imagined. And the cowboy standing beside her didn't seem like he wanted to help her.

Sloan let out a groan, knowing he was about to make a huge mistake and most likely, he'd regret it. "If you'll behave yourself, I'll take you into town myself."

"I'll be good." Rain began to think that maybe she'd jumped the gun on worrying.

"Since you're dressed like a man, I might as well let you ride with me." Sloan swung up into the saddle, then he reached down and before Rain knew it, she was sitting in front of him on the saddle. "Are you alright?"

"Yes." It was the most she could say. She'd got a glimpse of his deep blue eyes when he'd reached down to grab her arm. This was beginning to look like a dream she had. "My name is Rain Granger." Rain said, wanting to hear his and if it was what she dreamed, then surely, she'd fall off the horse.

"Sloan Weatherby."

Rain began to feel faint, "Did you say, Sloan?" Surely, she'd heard him wrong.

"Yes, is there a problem?" Sloan bunched his brows.

"No, there's not a problem." Rain straightened her spine, feeling like maybe she was in a dream.

For the rest of the ride into the small western town, Rain watched the scenery go by. There was nothing for miles in either direction except trees, dry dusty terrain and mountains. She didn't see any houses or sign of life. As they rode into town, several people stopped to stare at the couple. Some of the women put hands over their mouths in shock and the men smiled a little too broad.

"Why are these people staring?" Rain said, pushing back into the safety of the man behind her.

Sloan noticed her defensive move and it did something to him that he couldn't explain. "It's the way you're dressed. Women don't dress that way here." His voice a whisper against her ear.

"Oh." Rain looked down at her clothing, then back up at the women on the walkway. "It's all I have." Then she realized her other problem, she didn't have any money to buy any clothes. She hadn't thought this through.

"And no money to buy any either, am I correct?" Sloan said, tipping his hat to the sheriff as he rode past him.

Rain stuttered slightly, her lip trembling. "You're correct."

Without any warning, Sloan turned his horse toward a storefront at the end of town. Then he slid down out of the saddle. "Come with me." Sloan said, grasping her hand and pulling her down. She lost her footing when she landed, falling against his rock-hard chest. For a moment they stared at one another, then she backed up a little.

"Sorry." Rain felt like an outcast. But at least on this end of town, there wasn't anyone staring at her.

They walked inside the general store where an older gentleman came out of the back room. "Sloan, I wasn't expecting you until tomorrow."

"Well, I ran out of flour and thought I'd come into town earlier. Thomas, this is Miss Granger. The stagecoach had a little mishap and she lost everything she owned. So, I need to purchase a dress and..." Sloan turned to look at her again. "Some lady items too."

Thomas grinned, then looked at Rain too. "I think we can arrange that. Is she family?"

Sloan knew that this was a small town and to keep her reputation in check, he'd best make up a story. "Yes, this is my niece."

Rain's eyes shot up to question Sloan's words, but his eyes told her to keep quiet. She walked around, looking at the items on the shelves. This was like something out of a book. There was lamp oil, candle wax, lye soap and to her delight, lavender soap. She picked it up to inhale the beautiful aroma.

Sloan took it out of her hand and put it on the counter, "And this too." Then he gave her a wink.

Once the items were purchased, Sloan handed Rain the package that was wrapped in brown paper. "Go through that curtain and change into these."

Rain did as she was told, feeling a little out of place. But when she untied the bundle, she was glad to see that the dress was at least pretty. She pulled the sweater over her head and discarded her jeans, then stepped into the dress. It was a bit large, but it would have to do. She pulled on the petticoat, not sure how it worked, but doing the best she could do. Rain wrapped her modern clothing in the paper and neatly tied it. Since there were no shoes in the package, she kept on her ankle boots.

Sloan was leaning against the counter talking with Thomas when she came back up the aisle. He almost swallowed the piece of hard candy he'd just put in his mouth. In the soft blue and white striped dress, she looked even more like an angel. "I see it fits."

"It's a little big, but that's fine." Rain smiled. The dress was soft, and it flowed around her ankles as she walked. The petticoats swished back and forth with a soft sound. "Thank you."

"What do you think uncles are for?" Thomas said with a laugh.

Sloan rolled his eyes, then grabbed the grain bag full of groceries from the counter. "Thanks Thomas. I'll see you in a couple of weeks for those seed and some oats."

"See you then. Nice to meet you Miss Granger."

"Nice to meet you too." Rain said with a smile, then followed Sloan back to the horse. "So, where do I find lodging?" She said, looking up and down the walkway.

Sloan continued tying the bag to the horn of the saddle. "The way I see it, you don't have any money, so how are you planning to pay for lodging?"

"I'll figure something out. It's my only choice." Rain mumbled.

"Well, you don't look like the type of woman to work in the saloon, so I don't know what you're planning to do." Sloan climbed up into the saddle. "Come on. You can come to the ranch with me. I can use someone to cook and clean."

At first Rain just stared up at him, then she realized that she had no choice. "Alright, but I plan to work to repay you for all of your help and the clothing."

"Fair enough." Sloan pulled her up to sit side saddle this time. In the dress, she didn't need to be hiking it up and straddling the horse. He'd never get back in the good graces of the townspeople if he allowed that."

Chapter 2

The ride to Sloan's ranch took almost an hour. By the time Sloan slid down from the saddle, Rain's backside was numb, and her legs had been asleep for the last fifteen minutes.

"I don't think I can get down." Rain said, wiggling her toes to get some feeling back in them.

"I'll help you." Sloan reached up and grabbed her under her arms, pulling her down to stand on the ground. The moment he let go of her, she collapsed, but he managed to catch her before she hit the ground. "Good grief woman." Then he swung her up into his arms and walked to the front door of the ranch house.

One of Sloan's men came around the corner of the house just as Sloan stepped up on the porch. "Boss, you done got hitched." The man had a silly grin on his face.

Sloan looked down at Rain in his arms. "As a matter of fact, I did."

Rain's mouth fell open, "Sloan." She exclaimed.

"So, tell the men that we'll have a celebration dinner tonight." Sloan said, grinning as Rain hit him on the shoulder.

"I go from being your niece to becoming your bride. This is getting out of hand." Rain said as he placed her on the bench just inside the door.

"The men here know that I don't have any family left after the typhoid epidemic from a couple of years ago, so I can't tell them you're my niece."

Sloan went back to the horse to grab the sack of supplies.

The man was still standing by the horse. "I'll take the horse to the stables so that you can spend time getting your new bride settled in."

"That would be nice." Sloan had to admit that he was enjoying this. When he'd said she was his bride, it at least got her to stop talking.

Sloan walked back in the door and she wasn't sitting where he'd left her. He found her in the kitchen. "Are you hungry? When is the last time you had anything to eat?" He said as he saw her looking around the shelves.

Rain thought for a moment. "It's been a while. Probably last evening's dinner." That would explain why she was starving.

"I have salted beef in the cellar which is through that door there. There's some bread on the cutting board by the sink." Sloan said, putting away the bags of sugar and flour.

"Thanks for everything." Rain said as she cut a thick piece of bread, then slathered it with the jelly from the jar beside it. "This is good jelly. What kind is it?"

"Apple, from the tree out back. The cook in the bunkhouse loves to make jelly." Sloan brushed past her to get the salted meat.

When he came back up out of the cellar, she was sitting at the table. "I'm sure you're tired. You can sleep in the room just through that door." Sloan pointed at a door across the hall from the kitchen.

"Thanks. But I'm not tired." Rain wanted to explore this place. She's always dreamed of living on a ranch.

Sloan rolled his eyes, knowing he had his hands full with this one. "Ok, but don't get in any trouble." Sloan's words held a warning.

"What kind of trouble could I get in if I just go exploring?" Rain asked between bites of bread.

"Let's just say, you're outnumbered here. This is a working ranch with only men. Just stay in the house, please." Sloan said, pulling his hat down over his eyes.

"But I wanted to..." Rain closed her mouth when he cut his eyes at her. "I'll stay in the house."

"Good girl." Sloan said, then started for the back door.

"Where are you going?"

Sloan let out a long breath. He wasn't a patient man and couldn't understand why he made the decision to help this woman. "I have a ranch to run."

"So, what do I do while you're gone?" Rain said.

Sloan turned, not realizing she was standing just behind him. He jumped back. "Woman, you need to make your presence known. Now, since I'm giving you room and board, you need to earn it, one way or another." Sloan knew how that sounded, but he figured if he put a little fear in this woman, maybe she'd behave herself.

"Excuse me." Rain put her hand on her chest, taking a step backwards.

"Make sure that me and my men have three good meals a day and keep the house clean, then we'll do just fine." Sloan tipped his hat to her, then walked out the door, letting it slam shut behind him.

"Well, I guess I need to figure out how to cook and fast." Rain said with a frown. She went into the storage room to see what she had to work with and was happy to find a recipe book. After she looked through it, she knew trouble was coming. How was she supposed to understand all of this?

For a few minutes, Rain stared out the window at the barns. She wanted to go explore them, but she knew better. Once she got used to him, she'd take her chances. But for now, she'd behave herself. He didn't look like he'd harm her, but she didn't know him well. She'd watched people on television make biscuits, so surely that wasn't that hard. With a determined walk, she grabbed the flour and lard from the storage room.

Then she went down into the root cellar in search of milk. That's where it was kept in some of the books she'd read. She was happy to discover it was there.

After grabbing a bowl, she poured some flour in and put a generous handful of lard. Then started mixing with the milk. Before long she had a large ball in the middle of the bowl. Now how did she turn the stove on. Since there were no knobs, she didn't have a clue as to how to work it. Then she remembered that she had to put wood in it. Looking around, she found a wooden box by the back door that held several sticks of wood, so she filled the stove up and waited. When it started heating up, she placed the pan of biscuits in the oven and went to explore the rest of the house.

The house was relatively clean, which surprised her. She walked across the hall to the room that Sloan said she could use. It was a nice room with a large window. There was a full-sized bed, a dresser with a mirror on the wall and a wardrobe where she could hang her clothes. Then she thought about it, she had no clothes. That would be a problem and soon.

She left the bedroom to explore the rest of this large house. Rain was intrigued by the furniture that would be considered antiques in her world. The den was simple with a couch and rocking chair that set by the rock fireplace. Out of habit, she reached for the light switch, but giggled when all she found was bare wall.

There was a dining room across the hall from the den that looked to be where the men of the ranch met. It needed a woman's touch, that was a fact. The long handmade table would sell for thousands in a store in her time. She ran her hand over the polished wood, amazed at the work that must have went into making this table. There was a cabinet against the wall that held plates and cups.

Once she was back in the wide entrance, she gazed at the stairway, wondering if she dared explore up there. Then curiosity getting the best of her, she took the steps with excitement. She reached the landing which opened into another wide hallway. To her left was a single door, then across from her was another door and to her right one last door. She opened the one to the left first, finding a bedroom which had to be Sloan's. The bed was unmade and there were clothes hanging on a chair by the wall. She walked in and pulled the sheets up, then the coverlet. His masculine scent drifted up as she fluffed the pillows. It was a pleasant mix of spice and leather, which made her smile with pleasure.

Rain walked out to explore the room at the end of the hall. She was surprised to find a large claw foot tub. Of course, there were no handles, which intrigued her. If she desired a bath, would she have to haul water from the well?

The last door led to a stairway. At first, she just stared up into the darkness, unsure if she should explore any further. Then the scent of something burning made her turn from the stairs to look around for the source. As she started down the stairs, she heard the backdoor slam shut as someone came in. That's when it hit her, the biscuits. With a gasp, she ran down the stairs and into the kitchen to find Sloan pulling the blackened pan out of the oven, tossing it on the table with a grunt.

"Woman, don't you know to watch what you're cooking? Where were you?" Sloan's eyes met hers in frustration.

"I was only gone a moment. How could they burn so quick?" Rain shrugged, not sure what had happened.

Sloan put his hands on his hips, trying to calm his heart from racing out of his chest. "You put way too much wood in the stove, and it could've burned the house down. I think I lost one of my lives when I saw the smoke billowing out the back door."

"Oh, it wouldn't have burned the house down." Rain said with a roll of her eyes. "Don't be so dramatic." She was used to talking to her friends, but this man was another thing entirely as she was about to find out.

"Lady, this is my house. I would like for it to stay standing." Sloan took a deep breath as one of the men ran into the back door, sliding to a stop when he saw Rain.

"Howdy ma'am." The man said, tipping his hat to her. "Looks like we'll be eating salted meat sandwiches tonight." The man said with a frown.

"I'll get something fixed, just go back to what you were doing." Sloan said, not happy with the way the man was staring at Rain. He'd have his hands full with her here. Once the men got a good look at her, they'd be wanting to stay at the house, and he wouldn't get any work out of them. That was if she didn't burn the house down first.

"Do you know how to cook?" Sloan said in a huffy tone.

Rain looked down at the toe of her shoes, knowing there was no sense in lying now. "A little."

"A little. Well, that's not going to help with this evenings meal." Sloan walked down to the cellar and came back with some salted meat and a couple of potatoes. "Can you at least peel these?" He handed her the potatoes.

"Yes, I can peel potatoes." Rain snatched them from his hands and turned her back on him. He thought she was stupid. Anybody could peel potatoes. She took the knife that he handed her.

"And try not to cut any fingers off in the process." Sloan ground out as he turned back to the meat. A grin crossed his handsome face as he saw her rigid posture. She was furious with him. There was nothing like an angry woman.

Before long, Sloan had fried up some of the meat and then sliced the potatoes in the grease. The potatoes fried up nice and golden brown, the aroma filling the house. Rain's stomach began to growl with hunger as she watched him put the fried potatoes on a platter.

Sloan pointed toward the back door, "Go out on the porch and ring the bell. The men will be hungry and ready to eat by now."

Rain did as she was told, pulling the bell. The loud ringing made her headache. She'd need to learn some cooking skills and soon or Sloan would send her packing. And the thought of having nowhere to go had her feeling a little scared. Now she wondered if she'd done the right thing by slipping back in time.

Chapter 3

Rain stood at the sink, washing dishes in the water she'd heated on the stove. She watched the men as they walked back to the bunkhouse. They seemed nice, but some of them made her feel uncomfortable. Sloan was watchful of how they treated her. Of course, the men thought she was his new wife. Several congratulated them when they walked in for dinner. It made her feel strange, but Sloan tried to make it as easy as possible. Once he even put his hand over hers, just to make it more believable.

She turned to place a plate in the rack that sat by the sink, noticing someone behind her. Sloan was leaning in the doorway, watching her. "What? Am I washing the dishes wrong?" Rain said in a sassy tone.

Sloan grinned, "You are washing them just fine." He said as he took a step toward her, but then he stopped. "Where were you headed on the stage?" Ever since he'd rescued her from the runaway stage that morning, he'd been interested in where she was headed all alone. And where she'd come from. It was like she breezed into her life on a cloud and left him feeling strangely unbalanced.

Rain wiped her hands on the towel by the wash basin, then turned her eyes toward Sloan. She knew that telling him the truth would have her on a train to who knows where in a matter of minutes. So, she had to make it believable. With that thought, she pulled from the latest western historical romance she'd been editing.

"I was all alone now that my parents were both gone. It was too disheartening to stay there in the house we shared. Then I accepted a proposal from a young man in town. It didn't take long to figure out that he just wanted to marry me for my parent's money. He didn't realize that my father had squandered away the family fortune at the gambling table in the local saloon. But when he figured it out, he made it bad for me to stay in town. He spread nasty rumors about me, so I did what I had to do. I booked a trip on the stage going west and never looked back."

Sloan crossed his arms across his chest, not believing a word she said. He was a good judge of character and this woman didn't seem the type to just run off on her own. "So, where were you planning to go?"

Rain shrugged her shoulders, seeing the distrust in his eyes. She hated lying to him, but until she knew him better, it was her only choice. "I figured I would know home when I found it."

"And you think you've found it?" Sloan raised a brow, beginning to wonder if he needed to close his eyes tonight for fear of who this woman was. And another thought went through his head, if she was telling the truth, who would be coming after her. Then he gave her a long look and knew that no man in his right mind would let this woman go. There was more to her story and he intended on finding out.

"Maybe." Rain stared out the window, knowing deep down in her heart that she had found it. There was a feeling that went through her as she gazed out at the barns, and the surrounding land. And then there was the ruggedly handsome cowboy that was staring holes in the back of her head. She felt a tug every time she looked at him.

"So, when are you planning to tell me the truth." Sloan squinted at her, wanting to know the truth. Was she running from an abusive man? Was she running from the law? "Or do I need to take you to catch the next stagecoach now?"

Rain whirled around her eyes large with fear. "Oh, please don't do that." She exclaimed.

"Then be straight with me. I don't take kindly to people that don't know how to speak the truth." Sloan said in a deadly serious tone that was just above a whisper.

"If I tell you the truth, will you at least give me the benefit of the doubt?" Rain began to wring her hands together in front of her.

"I'm listening." Sloan pulled out a chair to sit down as she told him another tale.

With a deep cleansing breath, she began. "You see, my great, great grandmother, Marina, well, she was a witch." Rain held up her hand when he started to stand up. "Just listen. She put a spell on three journals. One for each of my sisters, and myself. It would send us back in time to find our..." She couldn't say true love, or she'd have him running in the opposite direction. "To find our destiny or place in this world."

Sloan held up his hand, "Wait a minute. Are you saying that you traveled here on a witch's spell?"

"Yes, well, sort of. You see, all I had to do was write in the journal and the spell would know where I belonged."

"So, how did you end up in the runaway stage?"

"I guess that's where I landed." Rain knew he didn't believe a word she said.

"Landed?" Sloan stood up, running his fingers through his hair. "Are you saying that you're a witch?" He'd heard of witches, but only in fairy tales and legends. Now, he had a self-proclaimed fairy tale living in his house, great, just great.

"No, that was my ancestor. I don't have any special powers that I know of." Rain sat down at the table, feeling light-headed from all of this. "She was a healer, not a witch in the bad sense."

"A healer? Like a witch doctor?" Sloan was having trouble with this new story. The first story was more believable. "I think your first story was more believable."

Rain knew that she was losing this situation and quick. "Look, I'm telling you the truth. I don't know how it works, but I do know that one minute I was in New York and the next, I was in a runaway stagecoach."

Sloan rolled his eyes. "Let's assume you're telling the truth. How did you achieve this time travel experience?" He had to admit, he was curious. It was no secret that there were things in this world that he didn't understand. Maybe this was one of them. But he doubted it.

"I wrote in the journal and poof, I was here." Rain said with a grin as a giggle erupted. Her story did sound outrageous.

A smile crossed Sloan's handsome face as her giggles became contagious. "So, poof, you were here. I don't think that's possible. And if it was, why would you be in a runaway stagecoach. It doesn't make sense. What were you writing in the journal that you say put you here?"

Rain blushed, the words she'd written coming to mind. This man standing before her was everything she'd ever wanted in a man, but she couldn't tell him that. She also couldn't tell him that it was about the person they were meant to spend the rest of their lives with.

"I'm waiting." Sloan murmured.

"I wrote that I wanted to be on a ranch in the 1800's." Rain rushed the words, not looking him the eyes.

"And?" Sloan knew she was holding back something.

"It's just been a dream of mine since I was a little girl and read books about the west during this time period. I've always fantasized about it." Rain shrugged her shoulders. She told him the truth, well, most of it.

Sloan growled, "Lady, this is a little far-fetched for me. I don't know what or who you're running from, but just don't let it affect anything here at my home. I'll let you stay here, but the minute you cause any trouble, I'll be taking you to catch the next stagecoach."

"I promise there will be no trouble and I'll do my best to learn how to cook." Rain said, trying to reassure him that it would be alright.

"If what you say is true, what happens if you want to go back to your own time? How do you manage that?" Sloan couldn't help but ask. This woman intrigued him and that was bothersome. He didn't have time to deal with a woman right now, but here she was.

That's when Rain remembered the journal. Where was it? She remembered clutching it as things started spinning at her apartment. "Did you happen to see my journal when you rescued me? I'll need it to get back to my own time."

"Are you ready to go back already?" Sloan asked, not sure why it bothered him to think that this woman that he'd only met a couple of hours ago wanted to leave.

"I'm just asking in case I decide to." Rain said in a lowered voice. She was unsure what would take place, but she wanted to make sure that she had a way home if she needed it.

"I don't remember seeing it, but I'll have one of the men ride into town tomorrow to check with the stage company. They have a box there for items found in the coaches."

"Thank you. That would be great."

Sloan pulled out his pocket watch, then moved toward the back door. "I need to go check the barn before I turn in."

"Alright. I'll just put these dishes away." Rain said, then she looked outside and realized it was already dark. "What time is it?"

"Just after 7." Sloan said, placing his hat on his head.

"You're going to bed this early?" Rain said with a frown. She was used to staying up until midnight, usually reading.

Sloan let out a calming breath. This woman was full of questions. "I start my day well before daylight and turning in before 8 gives me enough sleep to make it through the next day of work."

"Oh, well, makes sense." Rain frowned. What would she do to get sleepy? "Do you have any books I can read?"

"Books?" Sloan opened the door but waited for her answer.

"You know, those things with lots of pages filled with stories." Rains answered in a sarcastic tone.

"Don't push it." Sloan ground out. "Look on the shelves in the front room. There are a couple of books in there."

Rain smiled, happy to know she would have something to do once he went to bed. "Thank you, Sloan." She turned to finish the dishes.

Sloan watched her for just a moment, then he walked outside. Having a woman in the house would be interesting. He just hoped she didn't burn his house down or rob him blind. Maybe he was taken with her beauty, but he was smart enough to know to keep an eye on her. There was something about the way she told her story that made him want to believe her. She seemed passionate about it. He'd give her a chance.

Chapter 4

Once she finished the dishes, Rain walked into the den to check out the books. She was happy to see at least a dozen or so books on the shelves. Thumbing through them, she saw that most were classics from way back. Then she grinned, they wouldn't be classics yet in this time period. Rain picked one that she'd read several times but was one of her favorites. As she opened it, she realized that it was a first edition. This was amazing. She inhaled the familiar smell of a paperback book.

Even back in this time, they smelled basically the same.

Rain sat down in the chair by the fire, struggling to read with just the firelight. There was a lantern on the table by the chair, so she decided to light it. She picked up a match out of the little wooden box by the fireplace. Sloan walked in as she touched the match to the wick on the lantern. It was up too far and when it flamed up too high, she jumped back, landing in his arms. For a moment he held her against his chest. Then realizing what he was doing, he stepped back.

"You have to be careful to adjust the wick." Sloan said as he lowered it to make the flame smaller. He'd just put in new wicks earlier that day.

"Thanks." Rain said as she sat down in the chair and opened the book. She pulled her legs up underneath her, spreading the large skirt around her legs.

"I'll get some more logs for the fire. It looks to be a cold night." Sloan went out the door and came back a moment later with an armload of logs.

"I love the fire. My apartment at home is heated with a furnace." Rain said, not thinking that he wouldn't know what a furnace was. Then she saw his confused stare. "Oh right, you wouldn't know about those. It's an electric heating system that flows through the house. There are pipes and vents throughout the apartment that carry the heated air."

"Great idea." Sloan said with a frown.

Rain watched as he stoked the fire, then placed a decorative screen in front of it to keep the sparks at bay. Once he finished, he sat down in the chair opposite her. At first, he was quiet, then he turned to look at her. "What time do you go to bed in New York?"

"Around eleven or so." Rain said with a smile.

"That late. Don't you have to get up and start your day early? Surely you don't let your horses wait that long to feed." Sloan was surprised at her bedtime.

Rain laughed, "I don't have horses in New York. I have a car, or I take a bus. And my office doesn't open until eight, so I usually sleep until six thirty."

"If you don't own a horse, how do you get around?" Sloan leaned forward, propping his elbows on his knees. He couldn't help but want to know more about this mysterious world that she spoke of.

"As I mentioned, I have a car. It's a mode of transportation that hasn't been invented yet in your time. It has four wheels and an engine runs it." Rain grinned as he looked at her strangely.

For a few minutes he let that soak in, then he looked at the fire. "It's the best part of the evening when I sit down to watch the fire."

"Don't you get lonely here all alone." Rain closed the book, watching him in fascination. He was such a handsome man. Why wasn't he married?

"I'm not alone. I have the men and my animals." Sloan said, not looking toward her. He didn't want to admit it, but he did have moments when he longed for a wife to spend time with. Especially when darkness crept in. Some nights seemed to last forever in the quiet house.

Rain couldn't help but feel sorry for Sloan. He seemed sad as he stared into the fire. Was there someone in his past that he was thinking about? This man had to have local ladies beating down his door. "Wasn't there ever a time when you had a lady in your life?"

Sloan looked up at her, their eyes colliding. "Once upon a time I had a lady in my life, but she was taken from me during the smallpox epidemic two years ago."

"I'm sorry. Tell me about her." Rain wanted to know everything about this cowboy sitting in front of her. The cowboy had given her a chance, even with the amazing story she'd told him, he still let her stay here in his home. But what was his life like before she came here?

"Ruth was a sweet young woman with a heart of gold. We'd known one another all our lives. Our parents were friends, so it was natural that we'd get together. Or let's say, it was expected. We were best friends and when she grew of age to court, I did what was thought for me to do. I asked her on a buggy ride." Sloan seemed to lose himself in thought for a moment, then he continued. "I remember it as though it was yesterday. The sun was bright, and the skies were the bluest I'd ever seen. It reflected the blue in her eyes." Sloan cleared his throat, feeling like he'd opened his soul to a stranger, and it made him feel like a fool. "Anyway, we promised to marry one another, but the week before we were to wed, the smallpox hit the town. She was helping with the patients and contracted it."

"Sounds like she was a good woman." Rain said with a small smile.

"She was." Sloan said with a grunt. Then he stood up. "I'm going to bed now. Don't mess with the fire. I've got it set for the night." When he got to the door, Sloan didn't turn to look at her, but spoke his mind. "I may not believe the story of how you got here, but I believe everything happens for a reason." Then he was gone.

Rain listened as he went up the stairs, then crossed the little hallway to his bedroom. His words had touched her heart. With those words, she knew that he'd let her stay for as long as she needed to. Tomorrow she'd show him that he hadn't made the wrong choice. She opened the book and began to read.

Sloan walked into the den around midnight, wanting to make sure she'd blown the lamp out. He was surprised to see her laying in the chair, sound asleep. For a moment he just watched her, wondering why she'd been put in his life. As he'd laid in his bed, sleep not seeming to come, his mind had drifted to the beautiful woman sitting in his den. When he saw the runaway stage, he'd been headed toward town for supplies. He heard her scream and knew he had to help. There was something about her that just made him want to see where this would lead. He didn't need a woman in his life, but maybe the man upstairs thought different. And the fact that she reminded him of Ruth was unsettling.

With careful steps, he walked over to look down at her. He couldn't just leave her in the chair, or she'd wake up with a stiff neck. Sloan knew he'd regret this, but he lifted her into his arms and started for her room. Just as he reached the hallway, she opened her eyes. "Go back to sleep. I'm just putting you in your room." And with those words, she closed her eyes. He didn't think she was fully awake, but he wanted to reassure her of his intentions.

Once he'd placed her on the bed, he pulled her boots off, then pulled the blanket over her. One last look at the beautiful woman that had mesmerized him, he walked out, leaving the door slightly open. Sleep would be a long time coming now. Her beautiful eyes filled his mind as he closed his eyes and the scent of lavender drifted up from his sleep shirt where he'd carried her in his arms. He'd never smell that scent again without thinking of her. When he finally went to sleep, his dreams were of her this night, not of his sweet Ruth.

Rain turned over in the bed, opening her eyes as a sound overhead woke her. At first, she thought it was her upstairs neighbor, but then as she listened for the usual morning sounds that filled her New York apartment, realizing where she was. It was silent other than the footsteps overhead. Sloan was up, which meant the men would be too. She got out of bed, not remembering how she got here last night. Maybe she walked in her sleep. She noticed a pitcher of water sitting on the corner of the dresser. There was a small washcloth and bar of soap in a tray beside it. Rain washed off then pulled on her clothes that she'd been wearing when she arrived. The jeans felt good on this cold morning.

Sloan was standing at the stove when she walked into the kitchen. He looked up, then did a double take. "No ma'am. You go right back in there and put on that dress. I will not have my men gawking at you in your indecent attire."

"But this isn't indecent. I'm completely covered up." Rain looked down at the clothing.

"Women do not wear men's trousers. It's not proper." Sloan turned back toward the stove, unable not to stare at her in the close-fitting pants. "I can't have you parading around like a saloon girl."

Rain's cheeks turned red at the comment. "This is what we wear in my day."

"Well, it may be proper for your day, but here you'd be frowned upon." Sloan said, not looking her way, but pointing toward her room. "Now get in there and dress yourself like a lady."

"Fine." Rain stomped into the bedroom, slamming the door with a screech. She changed into the dress that wrapped around her legs and made her uncomfortable. When she returned to the kitchen, Sloan turned to see that she had changed.

"Better." Sloan said with a grunt.

Rain went down to the cellar and grabbed some salted bacon strips. "Sloan, I didn't see the carton of eggs in the cellar. Where do you keep them?" Rain asked as she closed the cellar door.

"They are in the chicken house." Sloan raised a brow, not sure where else they would be.

"The chicken house?" Rain said, then thought about the books she'd read. "Oh right, the chicken house."

Sloan let out a long breath, "Come on, I'll show you where it is." He grabbed a basket that was hanging by the door. "Here, put this on." Then he handed her a jacket from a hook.

Rain slid her arms into the large buckskin jacket, feeling the warmth surround her. "This is a nice jacket. Did you buy it at the store in town?" She said as she ran her fingers over the soft material.

"No, I got it from the tribe on the other side of the mountain. I'm friends with the chief. His wife made this for me last winter."

"Nice." Rain began to think about the fact that Indians were also in the vicinity, hoping she got to see them.

Rain followed him in the dark. The chicken house was just below the house. As he unlatched the fence, he turned toward her. "Here, hold on to the basket while I gather the eggs. But watch what I do because starting tomorrow, this is your job."

Sloan moved a chicken off her nest of straw, pulling out two eggs. Then he repeated the action until all the nests were checked. "They produced well today. This should be enough for breakfast today and the next couple of days."

The men were already making noise in the bunk house when they crossed the yard, headed back to the house. Rain hoped that she could manage to make a decent breakfast for them.

Chapter 5

Rain outdid herself for breakfast, or so she thought. She scrambled eggs and fried bacon for the men. Then she sliced some bread from the loaves that Sloan left for her. Had he made this himself? The bacon turned out a little crispier than usual, but the men seemed to enjoy it. She noticed a couple of them putting pieces of eggshell on their plates, but none of them complained.

Sloan waited for the men to leave before he commented. "At least you didn't set fire to the oven this time. But in the morning, you can leave the shells out of the eggs." He tipped his hat, then walked out the door.

After she washed up the breakfast dishes, she went to make up her bed. Once she had her room tidy, she went up to make up Sloan's bed. His sheets were twisted up like he'd had a night of tossing and turning. She grabbed his clothes and folded them neatly on the dresser. Was there a washer here or was it too soon for those to be invented yet? She went in search of one in all the rooms but didn't find one. It would be something to ask Sloan about. This dress would need washing soon, but what would she wear while it dried?

She walked out on the back steps to toss out the dish water. As she stood looking around at the beautiful place that she now called home, she wondered if she'd ever see New York again.

Without the journal, there was no doubt that she'd never see it again, unless she found another way.

When her stomach started to growl, she realized that it was probably getting close to lunch time. She looked up at the old clock on the mantel and saw that it was eleven thirty. It was time to get lunch ready for the men. Rain sliced the remainder of the loaves of bread that were stored. Since Sloan had sliced up a ham from the cellar, she made sandwiches for the men. She sliced apples and placed them on the plate.

The men came in, talking and laughing, but they went silent when they saw her standing beside the table. Each of them tipped their hats, then waited for Sloan to come in behind them. He noticed the way the men were acting, so he looked her way, expecting to see the trousers again. She'd pulled her hair up in a high ponytail. Then he noticed that her bare toes were peeking from underneath her skirt. He turned to his men. "Go out back and wash up."

Once the men were gone, he took a step closer to Rain. "Remember when we discussed the trousers?"

"Yes, why?"

"Same goes for bare feet. I can see where it wouldn't look like such a big deal, but to these men, well, it is. So, could you put your shoes back on?"

"It's just feet for goodness sakes." Rain walked toward her bedroom not sure why bare feet were a problem. When she returned, the men were sitting at the table, quietly eating their sandwiches.

Sloan nodded his approval when she poked her foot out from under her skirt. The men were watching them, but when Sloan turned his eyes back to the table, the men looked away. Sloan knew they were trying to figure out the couple. Maybe it was the fact that they didn't act like a married couple. And he knew that if she was to stay here in the house with him and not be shunned by the ladies in town, then he'd need to make their marriage seem real, even though it wasn't.

"Sweetheart, can I have a little more tea?" Sloan said, feeling strange calling this woman sweetheart.

Rain whirled around in shock, not understanding the endearment. "Ok, sure." She poured him a little more tea is his almost full glass. Their eyes met and he nodded toward the men, then placed his arm around her waist. "Sloan?" Rain pulled back, but his held her tight.

"I thought maybe we could have dinner tonight, just the two of us. You know since we didn't get a proper honeymoon and all." Sloan said, smiling up at her.

That's when Rain caught on to his game. She decided to really pour on the act. With a slight turn of her hips, she landed in his lap. Sloan gasped, unsure of what was happening. "Oh darling, that would be wonderful." She said in a sweet tone, batting her eyes up at him.

Sloan was a little stunned by her behavior but was soon realized that she was adding to his game. Two could play at that game. "You know, the men can finish the rest of today's work without me, I might just stay here with my pretty little wife. What do you think about that?" Sloan said, staring into her eyes, daring her to go further with the game.

It was all the goading she needed. "I can't think of a better way to spend my afternoon then with my husband." She gave him a quick peck on his cheek, taking him by complete surprise.

The men cleared their throats, not sure how to react to the couples show of affection. Sloan and Rain were having so much fun playing this game that they didn't realize when the men left the room.

Rain started to stand up, but Sloan held her with his arm across her lap. Then he looked up to see the men were gone. "Where did they go?"

"I have no idea." Rain looked around, unsure of when they left. "I think the game went well enough to run them off." She giggled.

"Maybe so." Sloan scratched his head, then looked out toward the barn. "I guess now I have to stay in the house the rest of the day."

"It would seem so." Rain said as she picked up the empty plates and began to wash them.

"I'll dry while you wash." Sloan stood up and walked over to grab a towel.

"Thanks."

They cleaned the kitchen together in silence. Then as Rain draped the damp towel over the edge of the water bucket, she looked up at him. "So, what would you like to do this afternoon?"

"I'm not all that sure. I work every day so having an afternoon off is out of the normal for me." Sloan said, looking down toward the barn again.

"Why don't we go for a walk? I'd love to see more of this place." Rain said with hope.

"Alright, that sounds good and I can check the fences while we're out." Sloan said. "But let me get you a coat because there's a slight chill in the air."

When Sloan returned, he handed her a jacket that was made of a thick fabric with a lamb's wool liner. "Thanks."

They walked out the back door and started down the road that led by the barns. "Hold my hand until we get out of sight of the barn." Sloan grasped her small hand in his as they walked. It was not until they were well out of sight when Sloan realized they were still holding hands. He pulled his from hers, feeling a little lost without her small hand in his.

"Is all of this your land?" Rain pointed across the pasture, toward the open land beyond the fences.

"As far as your eyes can see." Sloan said with pride. "I'm the third generation to own this land. Although I did buy an additional amount of property."

"It's just beautiful." Rain smiled as they continued to walk through a grove of trees. When they came back out into open fields, she was delighted to see a couple of deer sprint across and jumping the fences not far from them.

Sloan watched her face as it lit up with excitement. He had to admit, she wasn't boring. There was another thing bothering him and that was what he'd read in her journal. His worker retrieved it from the lost and found at the stage company office. Who was she and why was she searching for the perfect cowboy to spend her life with? Was she a fortune hunter? If so, she'd picked the wrong man to cozy up to. For now, he'd keep the journal with him. The journal might be the key to figuring out what she was up to. Then again, somewhere in the back of his mind, he believed her when she said it was her way back home. And he wasn't ready to let her go just yet.

"There's a place just up ahead that we can stop and sit for a while." Sloan said as they continued once the deer went out of sight.

Rain just smiled, enjoying this time with him. Even with his gruff composure at times, he was a softy in her opinion. In the last couple of days, she grown fond of him, but in some ways, she missed New York. She missed electricity and running water most of all. Also, she wanted to take a long hot bath.

"Sloan, I saw the big tub upstairs at the house. Can I take a hot bath tonight?" Rain asked with her fingers crossed. She felt dirty and knew her hair needed washing.

Sloan almost tripped when she asked. "I can arrange that." He hadn't thought about the fact that she was a woman and probably would like to take an actual bath.

"Is it too much trouble?" Rain thought about the fact that they'd need to heat the water and carry it up the stairs to fill the tub.

"No. I'm sorry I didn't think of it earlier." Sloan said as he pushed on a leaning fence post to check it.

The moment they arrived at one of Sloan's favorite places, Rain knew. She gasped as the world opened up and seemed endless. "This is beautiful." There was a little pond with a couple of willow trees that had branches dipping into the cool water. It was like something out of a fantasy. Rain was drawn to a place just beside the water's edge where the grass was lush, and the willow trees offered shade. "I can imagine sitting on that rock over there, my feet dangling in the water on a warm summer day." Rain closed her eyes as she saw it vividly in her mind.

Sloan watched her. He had to step back from her when his mind imagined the scene she'd described. His imagination went to her sitting there too, but his view was of her with children playing in the grass and edge of the water. But who's children could he be imagining? He shook his head to clear that vision. This wasn't in his plans and he needed to readjust his thinking. She was a beautiful woman, but Sloan wasn't ready for more than just friendship with her.

Rain turned her head to see why he was so quiet. He was staring out across the pond, lost in thought. "Penny for your thoughts."

When their eyes locked, neither of them said a word. They just gazed at one another. There was something between them, whether it was friendship or something more, both were taken aback with the intensity of the moment. Sloan was the first to look away as he saw more than he wanted to see in her eyes. He had a bad feeling that in the end, she'd be hurt. Sloan was a difficult man and he knew that. He wasn't the romantic type nor was he a patient man. It surprised him when he told her to come back to the ranch with him after just meeting her.

"Let's get back to the house." Sloan said, needing to put some space between them. Just being here in his special place with her made him over think things. It also reminded him of Ruth and losing her. He just couldn't go through that again.

Rain was sad to leave the beautiful place so soon, but she saw a change in Sloan that told her more than words could. They'd taken a huge step today, but in just the short few minutes, they were stepping backwards.

Chapter 6

Rain walked through the back door ahead of Sloan. The walk home was quiet, both in deep thought. Rain was considering finding a way back to New York and Sloan was wondering if he should give her the journal so she could go back where she belonged.

"I'll get some wood and build a fire. There's a chill in the air. We may have a cold night ahead." Sloan mumbled, then he was out the back door, leaving her standing there.

Since the men were eating at the bunkhouse, Rain thought about cooking something special for Sloan. She walked down to the root cellar to see if there was any ham left. Sloan didn't come back through the back door with the wood. She heard him when he came through the front door. Was he avoiding her?

She managed to fry a couple of slabs of ham without burning them. As an afterthought, she grabbed a couple of potatoes and sliced them, then fried them in the juices from the fried ham. The biscuits she made seemed to do somewhat better, but the tasting would be the test.

Rain went in search of Sloan once dinner was done. She found him staring into the fire. "Sloan, I've got dinner ready."

"Alright, I'll go wash up." Sloan walked by her without a glance.

Sloan sat down at the table a few minutes later, "This looks good. Thank you." He managed to say, his mind on his decision from earlier.

"Don't thank me until you taste it." Rain said with a lopsided smile.

He picked up a biscuit. "At least they're not burnt."

"Nope."

Sloan brought the biscuit to his mouth, then tried to take a bite. It was hard as a rock. "They are a little hard." He tried to hide his smile.

Rain picked hers up and tried to bite it. "Oh no. Why can't I get this right?" She slammed it back on her plate in frustration.

"It takes practice for biscuits. After we eat, I'll give you a few pointers." Sloan smiled for the first time since their walk.

"Thanks." Rain felt like she'd failed again.

"The potatoes and ham are delicious." Sloan said around a mouthful of potato.

Rain smiled, glad that at least something went right. "I filled a couple of large pots for water. Will it take long to fill the tub upstairs?"

Sloan lifted his head, "I think I'll get the men to pull the smaller tub into the den by the fire. The house is too cool for the one upstairs right now."

"Oh, don't go to that much trouble. It's not that important." Rain said with a sigh. She'd been looking forward to losing herself for a while in a warm bath.

"It's not too much trouble." Sloan said. "Now, eat before your dinner gets cold." He snapped, feeling a little out of sorts now.

After dinner, Sloan went to get the men to help with the tub while she washed dishes. The pots of water were beginning to bubble by the time she heard the men coming through the front door. Rain walked in to see the large metal trough looking tub that had a slanted back. The two man that was helping Sloan with the tub looked up at Rain with a huge smile.

"Thanks for bringing it in." Rain said, walking over to look at the deep tub. How much water would she need?

"No problem ma'am. Hope you enjoy your bath." The man tipped his hat at her, then walked back out the front door with a huge grin.

"What's so funny?" Rain asked when she saw the strange look on Sloan's face.

Sloan ran his hand over his face, "Nothing that concerns you."

Rain closed her mouth, not saying another word. She turned and went into the kitchen to check the water. For some reason tears pricked the corners of her eyes. Sloan wasn't happy for some reason and she had a feeling that reason was her.

"Will two pots of hot water be enough?" Rain asked, not looking his way. She didn't want him to see the tears in her eyes.

"Yes. I'll start filling the tub with water, then we'll put the hot water in to see if you need more." Sloan brushed past her, going out the door again without even looking at her.

After the tub was almost halfway full, Sloan poured the hot water in. The steam coming up from the tub delighted Rain. "Do you have any soap I can use for my hair?" Rain asked in a timid voice, unsure of what was making him so quiet with her tonight.

"Let me go see." Sloan went upstairs, then a few minutes later, he came down and handed her a small bar of soap. "This was a present I'd purchased for Ruth, but she never got to receive it."

"I can't take that Sloan." Rains eyes met his.

"Just take it." Sloan pulled a towel from his shoulder and handed it to him. "Be careful and don't drown." He grunted as he walked back into the kitchen.

"Ok." Rain whispered as she walked into her bedroom to grab the undergarments, she'd washed out earlier and sat in the window to dry.

The soap was lavender scented, which was her favorite. She draped the towel over a chair beside the tub, then got undressed and slipped into the warm water. It was heavenly. She knew the water would get cool quick, so she lathered her body and hair first. Then she lay back to rinse the soap out of her hair. After she was certain all the soap was out of her hair, she leaned back against the curve of the tub and closed her eyes. Her body relaxed for the first time since she'd arrived here.

Sloan sat at the table, sipping coffee and trying to keep his mind off the woman in the den. Just the thought of her beautiful skin glistening in the firelight with droplets of water streaming... No, he had to get his mind in another place. The sloshing of the water had long stopped, and darkness had enveloped the house. The fire would be dying down and need tending soon. "Rain." Sloan called out from just inside the doorway of the kitchen. When she didn't answer, he became concerned.

With slow steps, he moved closer to the doorway of the den. "Rain?" But no answer. He walked into the den and saw the top of her head just below the rim of the tub. At first, he thought she'd drowned, then when he moved closer, he saw she was just asleep. Just as he turned his back on her, she opened her eyes, scrambling for the washcloth to cover herself.

"I'm sorry. The fire was dying, and you didn't answer my call... I thought... Dear heavens, I thought..." Sloan stammered, not knowing what to say. He could hear the sloshing of the water as she stood up and grabbed the towel to cover herself up. "I didn't come in here to... What I mean to say is, I just wanted to check on you." Sloan said with a gruff voice as he tried to clear his head.

"Sloan, it's alright. I'm covered now." Rain said with a giggle. He was from another time period, so of course she wouldn't just parade around in the buff, but it wasn't a big deal. The bubbles from the soap hid her body from his view when he first came in.

"I need to put some logs on the fire." Sloan skirted around the edge of the tub. Then out of the corner of his eyes he saw the flames reflecting over her smooth calves as she dried herself. He closed his eyes, trying to get that out of his head.

Rain shivered from the coolness of the air on her damp skin. "It has gotten cold in here." She said as she sat down on the edge of the hearth to watch him stoking the fire. The towel was wrapped around her, covering most of her body, but Rain felt vulnerable sitting here with Sloan. The fact that they were all alone in the house resonated.

Sloan turned to look into her eyes. The firelight dancing in them and on her skin. For a moment he was lost in their depths, then he shook his head. He couldn't let his body control him. The fact that he wasn't sure if it was just his body made him feel unsteady. "I'll go in the kitchen so you can dress in front of the fire." He rasped, unable to keep his eyes from her smooth shoulders and slender arms. With a shudder, he walked to the kitchen, grasping the back of a chair as he told himself to get control.

Rain moved to the chair where she laid her clothing. Her heart was clenching as she thought of the look that passed through his eyes. She knew he felt the same pull she did. If she had her journal, she'd have a way out and that would help her make up her mind about him. If she had that escape route and chose not to use it, then she'd know without a doubt that the feelings she had were true. After she dressed, Rain sat down on the hearth and ran her fingers through her long hair, letting it dry.

"Are you dressed?" Sloan called out from the hallway.

"Yes." Rain watched him walk into the room. He seemed to be on edge as he looked at her to confirm she was in fact dressed. "Did you think I lied to you?"

Sloan ran his fingers through his hair, not knowing what he'd thought. "What do you mean by that? You said you were, so I took you at your word." In frustration he forced the words out as he felt a lump forming in his throat. This woman was driving him insane. "I'll be back in a minute." He took the stairs two at a time. It was plain to see that if he didn't give her the journal, he'd go mad. This wasn't what he wanted, a woman living in his house. And if she was telling the truth about the time travel, then he couldn't ask her to stay. She didn't belong in this time period and it was getting more obvious by the day. He lifted his mattress and pulled the old leather journal out, holding it to his chest. Could he really do this? Was he prepared to let her go? Then he thought about the feelings he had when she was sitting by the fire, her skin glistening... With a groan, he sprinted back down to the den.

Chapter 7

Rain jumped to her feet when he rushed in with the journal in his hand. He put it in her hand but didn't let go at first. "I can't do this anymore. You're not what I need in my life and the longer you stay, the harder it will be to let you go." Sloan said in a rush of words that left him breathless. Their eyes were locked as she took the journal and clutched it to her chest. She'd thought it was gone forever.

"So, you want me to go." Rain's voice was a mere whisper as her heart began to beat hard in her chest. She wasn't prepared to let him go just yet. This is what she'd dreamed of, living on a ranch in the 1800's with a cowboy just like Sloan. But it was more than that. The man that stood before her was the exact man from her dreams. She knew that this was her destiny, but could she force him to accept that?

Sloan turned his back on her, unable to answer her question. So, he answered her with a question of his own. "Do you want to go?" He closed his eyes, waiting for what seemed like a lifetime for her to answer him.

"No." Rain whispered, tears forming in her eyes. "Sloan, I'm lost. I feel like my whole world is upside down. This is what I've dreamed of since I was a little girl. And now, here I am, living my dream. But if you want me to go, I'll go."

"Read to me what's written in the journal. I've read it, but I want to hear it from your mouth." Sloan said, turning back around to face her.

"Alright." Rain opened the journal with shaky fingers. She began to read. "The man of my dreams has long since died and the sorrow in my heart only deepens with each passing day. I know he's out there, waiting for me to join him. But I'm scared that when I find him, it will be too late." She closed the journal, not wanting to see the look in his eyes. She'd been speaking of him and she was more certain of that that anything in her life.

"Who is this man that you speak of? Is it me?" Sloan said, unsure of why he was asking. This was nonsense. Time travel didn't exist, did it? Had she really come back in time to find him? He was nothing but a rancher.

Rain let her eyes go from his scuffed, dusty boots up his long legs and trim body to his amazing blue eyes. She got lost in them. All she could do was nod as the emotion of knowing that he was the one she'd written those words about. It hit her all at once. Sloan Weatherby was the cowboy that filled her dreams and tortured her soul.

Sloan couldn't help himself. He grasped her by the arms, pulling her to his chest. As he crushed his lips to hers, he began to realize that maybe he did want her to stay. His heart slammed into his ribs as he deepened the kiss, pulling her closer. The scent of lavender filled his senses as he reached up with one hand to run his fingers through her damp hair. This woman had put a spell on him, and he was afraid that maybe that's all it was. But for this one moment, he didn't care.

The kiss was long and soul reviving. Neither of them wanted it to end. Just as he wrapped his strong arms around her, the fire popped, startling them. Sloan stepped back, knowing he'd just sealed his fate. He couldn't stay away from her, nor did he want her to leave him. "Stay with me. Don't go."

Rain was surprised to hear this gruff, strong cowboy saying the words that made her heart sing with joy. "Are you sure?"

Sloan smiled, "I'm not sure about anything right now, except one thing. I want you to stay and let us figure this out. If it's meant to be, it will be."

His mother's own words came into his head. She'd

spoke of his relationship with Ruth in those words.

Sloan had been unsure, but those words had led him

to the truth. Even though he'd lost Ruth, they'd

shared a bond that was unbreakable.

"I'll stay." Rain said.

"If you stay, we have to come to an

agreement. Soon the men will figure out that we're

not husband and wife. They'll see that you don't

share my room." Sloan said.

"What's the agreement?" Rain said with a

frown. She wasn't certain what he was about to ask.

"I need for you to move into the room with

me. I'll sleep on the floor. I just don't want the men

to figure it out. If one of them happened to see you

coming out of that room, well, they'd know we

were living under the same roof, not married. It

wouldn't look good to the townspeople." Sloan

didn't care what the people in town thought about

him, but he didn't want them thinking less of Rain.

Rain was quiet for a moment, unsure of what he was asking of her. Then she gave him a good look, "Ok, so if I move into your room, you'll sleep on the floor?"

"Yes, you have my word." Sloan rasped.

"Sloan, we're adults. I have a good friend back in New York that has slept in the same bed with me. It's fine." Rain said with a grin.

At first Sloan was a little shocked, "I don't understand. You let a man that you weren't married to sleep in your bed?"

"There's nothing going on so what's the difference?" Rain was raised in a different world than Sloan, so she didn't see the problem that he did. Her friend Winston slept over when he was up too late editing. They were friends and neither saw any harm in him sharing the bed, but that's where it ended. She could see Sloan's mind turning. He was still having trouble with this.

"Sloan, there's no sense in you sleeping on the cold, hard floor. We're adults and I can tell you,

I'm not letting you across the middle of the bed, so tonight I'll move into your room." Rain went to her room and packed up her one set of clothes, then came back to the den. "Alright, let's hit the hay." She grinned as she turned toward the stairs. She'd messed with Sloan's mind and she was enjoying every minute of it.

Rain went into the bathroom first, of course she didn't have nothing but the camisole that Sloan bought her the first day she arrived. When she came out wrapped in a sheet, he gave her a strange look. "You didn't buy me a gown, remember?"

"Oh, yeah, right. We'll need to go into town and get you some more clothing." Sloan said, watching her climb into his bed. "And soon." Then he was shutting the door, leaving her alone.

Rain stared up at the ceiling, feeling somewhat strange up here. The bed was a lot more comfortable than the one in the bedroom downstairs. She listened for Sloan to come out of the bathroom. When he did, she giggled. He was still fully clothed. "Sloan, you can get comfortable. I'll put this pillow between us if that helps your feelings."

Sloan stared at her, then shook his head. "What kind of world do you live in?" Sloan blew out the lantern, making the room go dark. He pulled his pants off, then laid them over the chair, then unbuttoned his shirt, leaving it on top of the pants. When he slid into the bed, he was uncertain if sleep would ever claim him. "Goodnight Rain."

"Goodnight Sloan. Sweet dreams." Rain said as she rolled to her side, putting her back toward Sloan. "Don't let the bedbugs bite."

"Is that a problem in New York?" Sloan said, his back to her.

"In some places, but not my apartment." Rain said with a satisfied grin.

"What's an apartment?"

"It's like a small room in a large house. I rent it from the owner." Rain said, plumbing the feather pillow.

"Oh, alright. Kind of like the boarding house in town."

"Just like the boarding house."

They were both quiet for a while, then Sloan spoke, making her jump. "What's life like in New York?"

Rain smiled, turning on her back. "It's busy. There are building that scrape the sky they are so tall. And the traffic is horrendous, but I love the noise. The sidewalk vendors are interesting. I buy my coffee from one of them on my way to the office."

"Buildings that touch the sky. That's amazing." Sloan tried to imagine it. "And traffic, what's that?"

"Well, it where there are a lot of cars piled into the street at one time going in the same direction." Then she thought about it. "Oh, that's right, you don't have cars yet. Remember, I mentioned that I own a car, not a horse. It's my transportation."

"I do remember you mentioning that." Sloan laid there for a minute, looking out the window. "So, does anybody own a horse?"

"Sure. The stables out in the country have horses." Rain smiled, knowing she was blowing his mind.

"How can this life compare with that?" Sloan asked, realizing that he couldn't offer her much, compared to what she had in New York.

"You'd be amazed. There are times when my life is so crazy that I can't think straight. Then others, when I get so bored, I'm almost crazy from that. I love living there, but I've always dreamed of living somewhere like this. Does that make sense?"

"Maybe." Sloan turned to face her. "You're so different from the women I've known. It's a little disconcerting."

Rain turned to face him over the pillow. She could see his silhouette from the moonlight streaming in the window. "I hope that's not a bad thing."

"No. It's a little refreshing. I don't feel like I have to walk on eggshells with you." Sloan smiled into the darkness. He enjoyed knowing that she was just on the other side of the pillow. He'd worried about her being downstairs all alone.

"Just watch yourself. I have my limits." Rain said in a huff.

"Yes ma'am." Sloan rolled to his back, draping his arm over his eyes. "Goodnight again."

"Goodnight Sloan. And thank you for rescuing me."

"I'm glad I did." Sloan said with a rumble of laughter that vibrated in the quiet room.

"What's that supposed to mean?" Rain said with a slight giggle.

"Just go to sleep woman, you're keeping me awake." His grin was broad as he closed his eyes.

Rain closed her eyes. "You asked the question, I didn't."

They both laughed.

Chapter 8

Sloan slid out of bed before daylight, trying not to wake Rain up. He'd slept somewhat good but just the knowledge that she was in the bed beside him, well, it did something to him. He looked down at her for a moment, then he grabbed his clothes and went to the bathroom. When he was dressed, he went down the stairs to the kitchen and started the coffee.

One of the men came through the back door, "Boss, the mare that was due has started to foal. Thought you might want to know."

Sloan looked up at the ceiling, thinking of Rain asleep in his bed. He rubbed his chin, "I'll be out in a few minutes."

"Sure thing." The man said, then he looked up at the ceiling. "You're a lucky man."

"Thanks. I think so." Sloan thought about the man's words as he went back up the stairs to wake Rain. She might want to see the baby being born. She was still sleeping when he walked into the bedroom. He leaned over her, shaking her shoulder. "Rain."

Rain grumbled, then she opened her eyes. "What's wrong?" She mumbled.

"There's a foal coming. I thought you might want to see it being born." Sloan said.

Her eyes popped open wider. "For real?"

"For real." Sloan rolled his eyes. "Get dressed and you can go to the barn with me. I'll grab you one of my jackets. The air is cool this morning." He walked out of the room to the closet in the hallway.

Rain got out of bed, straightening it a little before she pulled on the dress. As an afterthought, she pulled on her jeans underneath the dress. If it was cold, that would be extra protection. She walked out to the hallway and Sloan handed her a thick jacket. "Thanks."

Sloan headed down the stairs as she put her arms in the jacket that held his scent. She took a long sniff, then followed him. Her stomach growled as they walked through the kitchen. "Here's a biscuit to hold you over."

"Thanks Sloan." Rain took the biscuit, eating it as she followed him to the barn. This would be the first time she'd seen inside the big barn. It made her feel excitement as she walked inside. There were stalls on the right side and hay stacked on the left side. It looked to have around a dozen or so stalls. Sloan walked to the third stall, then he stopped.

"How far along is she?" Sloan asked as he knelt beside the mares protruding belly.

"She's getting close." One of the men said, then he noticed Rain standing in the doorway. "Ma'am." He touched his hat with a smile.

The mare let out a moan, then seemed to relax as Sloan said soothing words to her. He rubbed her belly, then laid his head on her belly to listen. He motioned for Rain. "Come here."

Rain walked to his side, unsure of what he wanted her to do. "What?"

Sloan grabbed her hand, placing it on the mare's belly. "Feel the foal moving. It's out of room in there."

She smiled as she felt the life under her fingertips. When her eyes met Sloan's, there was something that passed between them. They both felt it and for a moment they just stared at one another.

Then the man on the other side of the mare cleared his throat.

"Let's get this foal born." Sloan said with enthusiasm. He always enjoyed new life born on the ranch.

Rain did as she was told, rubbing the Mare's neck and soothing her as Sloan and the other man helped the baby. It was a long process, but once the foal started into the world, he came quick. In a rush of fluid and furry baby horse, there it was. Rain wiped tears as she saw the baby stumbling to its feet. Life was amazing.

Sloan watched her as she smiled at the wobbly baby. He imagined when she had her first child, she'd smile like that. Then he shook his head. He had no right to think about that. But then again, maybe life was taking a turn for them both.

"Oh Sloan, thank you for allowing me to watch. That was so amazing." Rain said with a huge grin.

"I thought you'd enjoy that." Sloan helped her to stand. He didn't let go of her hand at first, then with a slow movement, he pulled his hand from hers. "I'll be back to the house in a few minutes to clean up and eat."

Rain took it as her dismissal. She walked up the house as the sun broke over the far mountains. The air was crisp on her face as she looked up at the purplish sky. This was something she didn't see much in New York. As she walked into the house, her heart was singing. She couldn't believe what she'd just witnessed, the beginning of a new life. Maybe it was a sign for her new life.

As she cooked breakfast, her mind was on the journal laying on the bedside table upstairs. She wondered what was happening in New York now. Had anyone missed her yet? Then she thought about Sloan and knew that she'd miss him if she went back. She wanted to give this life a chance, but was she truly prepared to give up her future life?

Sloan came in the door, seeing her in a lost stare. He stood in the doorway watching her for a moment. She was frowning, like her mind was a million miles away. "Is everything alright?"

Rain turned. "Yes, I guess I just slipped away for a moment. Breakfast is almost ready." She said absently.

Sloan knew that whatever she'd been thinking, it was sobering to her. Should he have asked her to stay? Was she longing for her life in New York? After breakfast, he'd have a talk with her. He didn't want to lose her, but he also didn't want her to stay if she didn't want to.

The men were all talking about the new foal, which looked to be healthy. They were laughing at the wobbly legs that seemed long and powerful. Sloan just smiled, nodding as they talked. Rain noticed his distance from the men's conversation.

Once the men were gone, Rain saw a change in him. He seemed to be uncomfortable and needing to talk. So, she grabbed the bull by the horns.

"Alright, what's wrong?" Rain poured him another cup of coffee, then sat down with her fresh cup.

Sloan looked at her for a long moment, seeming to memorize every aspect of her. "Rain be truthful with me. Are you missing home?"

Rain put her cup down, absently pulling at a string on her sleeve. "Sometimes. Why?" She couldn't look at him for some reason.

"I need to know if I'm keeping you from having the life you want. We don't have a commitment other than making the agreement last night." Sloan muttered.

"Sloan, do you want me to go back or to stay?"

"I want you to do what makes you happy." Sloan said, his eyes on her as he waited for her answer.

Rain stood up and stared out the window. "Sloan, I need to know something."

"Alright." He said.

"Will there ever be anything between us? Or rather, do you think that one day you could have feelings for me?" Rain had to know. If she was staying here only to cook and clean, then why bother. And the way he looked, she wondered about that.

Sloan cleared his throat, "Rain, when I lost Ruth, I shut my heart off. Then you came along and I began to wonder if maybe it was fate. But I can't compete with the men from your time period. I'm me and nothing else."

"I understand that. And I've never wanted one of them before. You see, my heart has always been set on finding a cowboy. A cowboy from the 1800's." Rain stared at him, letting that sink in.

His eyes found hers, then he reached out to grasp her hand. "So, are you saying that I'm what you've been looking for?"

"Yes Sloan, you're what I've been looking for." Rain nodded her head as tears pricked her eyes.

"So, let's make this official. Why wait?" Sloan stood up, pulling her to him. The kiss was tender and told of their feelings. "Rain, will you become my wife?" Sloan said, holding his breath.

"Only if we can move the pillow." Rain said, trying to hold a straight face.

Sloan growled, pulling her close for a heated kiss. "We'll move the pillow I can assure you of that." He picked her up, amazed that this woman that he'd only met a couple of days ago was going to be his wife. Was he rushing things? Maybe, but when things felt right, they felt right.

Rain felt true joy as he picked her up and spun her around. Was this too quick? She wasn't worried about that. This was what she'd always wanted. One look at Sloan and she'd known, deep down inside that he was the one.

"The circuit preacher will be in town today if you want to go get married. We can leave now and be in town to meet him when he arrives." Sloan felt like a young boy as excitement rushed through him. With Ruth, it had been something he'd always known. They would get married and have kids. He'd loved her, but the feelings he had for Rain were different. He couldn't breathe when he looked at her. She did something to him that made him feel more of a man. She made him feel like life wasn't right without her.

"Alright." Rain said with a grin. "Can we buy me a gown while we're in town?"

Sloan laughed, "We can buy you anything you want when we're in town."

"Just a gown and maybe another change of clothing. Especially since we've decided that I'm staying here." Rain put her tongue in her cheek as Sloan swung around to smile at her.

"You're right. You can't just wear that dress every day. And those pants under your dress won't do."

Rain pulled her skirt up, "But I thought I was making a fashion statement."

"I don't know what you're talking about, but no wife of mine will be wearing pants under her skirt." Sloan rolled his eyes. "I'll go tell the men that we will be out for the rest of the afternoon." Then as he started out the door, he looked a little sheepish. "Did you want to spend our honeymoon in town or here?"

"This is our home Sloan, so here." Rain shooed him out the door. She ran up the stairs to comb her hair and wash her face. Oh, what she wouldn't give to call her mother and sisters. But she couldn't do that. Just the thought made her a little sad, but they'd be happy for her.

The ride into town was long and dusty. Sloan drove straight to the little white church on the outskirts of town. The preacher had just arrived when they stopped at the front of the church. "Sloan, how have you been?"

"Never better preacher. This is Rain Granger. Rain, this is preacher Eli Golden."

"Nice to meet you Rain." The preacher said.

"We'd like to get married today." Sloan rolled off his tongue in almost one word.

"Well, let's get to it then." The preacher opened the door to the church and ushered them inside. "My caretaker can witness the nuptials."

Sloan and Rain stood holding hands as the preacher spoke from the Bible. They said their vows, smiling at one another like silly teenagers. When the preacher said he could kiss his bride, Sloan grasped her face between his large, work roughened hands and kissed her. After congratulations from the preacher, they walked up the sidewalk to the general store for clothes for Rain. She picked out a gown and another suitable dress for working on the ranch. Thomas, the store clerk, shook Sloan's hand and congratulated them.

Rain noticed a woman staying in the background, but she watched them as they walked out of the store. When Rain turned to look back at the doorway, the woman was peeking out the window. It made a shiver run down her spine.

Chapter 9

Sloan helped Rain down from the wagon when they arrived back at the house. He felt a little strange knowing they were now truly married and not just putting on an act for his men. As they walked up the walkway to the front door, neither of them said anything. He opened the door, then as an afterthought, he swung her up into his arms and carried her over the threshold. It was superstitious, but he wanted them to start off on the right foot.

"I guess I need to get dinner started. The men will be starving." Rain said, feeling shy.

"The men are eating in the bunkhouse tonight. I told them we were having a special night, so it's just the two of us." Sloan said. "I'll build a fire to get some of the chill gone if you want to grab a couple of biscuits and ham."

"Ok, sounds good." Rain went upstairs to put away her new dress and laid the gown on the bed. For a minute she stared at the bed. She was now Sloan's bride. That seemed strange, but like it was always meant to be. She smiled to herself as she walked back downstairs to fix their dinner.

Sloan walked into the kitchen just as she was pulling the ham from the iron skillet. "Smells good." He pulled two plates down and placed them on the table.

"Do you have any candles?" Rain said absently. She was thinking of a romantic dinner, then she turned to look at the lantern that was on the table, the flame dancing around.

"Candles?" Sloan said with a questioning look. "Do we need more light?"

"No, forget I said it." Rain blushed. "In my time, we light candles to make dinner more romantic."

"Oh." Sloan frowned. "I have a couple of candles, but they won't give off much light."

"Don't worry about it." Rain said as she sat down across from him.

They ate their biscuits and talked about their childhoods. Both were so different. He laughed when she told of the time she fell out of the tree and got twelve stitches. Then she smiled when he told about stealing his dad's tobacco and how sick he'd turned when he chewed it.

Once they cleared the dishes, Sloan put a couple of logs on the fire and sat down on the hearth. His mind was whirling with the fact that he'd just married a stranger. But the funny thing was, she didn't feel like a stranger at all. From the moment he saved her from the stagecoach, he'd felt as though they'd known one another forever.

Rain went upstairs to get comfortable. She was happy to have a gown to wear to bed. In New York on cool nights, she would change into her gown and sit beside her gas log fireplace. It was relaxing after a long day in the office. She pulled her hair down out of the bun she'd put it up in and let it flow over her shoulders. For just a moment she paused, thinking about the fact that she'd married Sloan. Had she jumped too soon? Then as her mind saw his face, and her heart fluttered, she knew she hadn't.

With slow steps, she walked back down the stairs and into the den where he sat staring into the fire. Sloan turned his head and locked eyes with her. He stood up, a gasp on his lips as he took a step toward her. Was she real? The glow of the fire reflected in her eyes, making her look mysterious. With her hair down, she looked like an angel in the white flowing gown. He took another step closer, trying to get a hold of himself. This was his wife. She was his.

Sloan closed the space between them, reaching out to grasp her arms. They stood, arms-length apart. "You look beautiful." His eyes roamed over her face, then down her body until his eyes reached her toes peeking out from under the hem of the gown.

"Thank you. I love the gown." Rain whispered. This was like something out of one of the novels she'd edited. Here she was, standing in front of the cowboy that was now her husband. With slow movements, she reached up and touched his cheek. "Am I dreaming?"

"If we are, I don't want to wake up." Sloan rasped, then he draped his arms around her, pulling her to his chest. He lowered his lips to hers, barely able to keep from crushing her in his strong arms as wave upon wave of emotion filled his soul. What he felt for this woman was powerful. Even though they hadn't said the words, he knew in his heart that they both felt it. He just wasn't ready to say he loved her.

But he'd show her that he did with each kiss tonight.

Rain wound her arms around his neck, running her fingers into the short hair at the back of his head. "Sloan."

"Yes." Sloan said, the words quiet in the dark room.

"This is real. This is what I came here for, this moment in time." Rain pushed up on her toes, letting her lips touch his in a tender kiss, but it was more powerful than the most passionate kiss. That one kiss spoke volumes of how she felt at that moment.

"I'm so glad that journal brought you to me. Please don't leave me." Sloan's words were like a match to the flame. He gathered her in his arms and crushed his lips to hers. It was as if he couldn't get close enough to her. With a shuddering breath, he reached down and swung her up into his arms. He moved toward the stairs, stopping at the bottom step and looking into her eyes. "Are you sure about this?"

Rain caressed his cheek, "Oh yes, I'm surer than I've ever been before."

Sloan needed no further words. He took her up the stairs and laid her on their bed. The moonlight streamed in the window as he knelt on the bed beside her. For just a moment, he hesitated, then he lowered himself to lay beside her, pulling her to him in a kiss that melted both their hearts.

The night seemed to stretch on as they shared their first night as husband and wife. As the moonlight moved across the bed, they held one another. Sloan never wanted to let her go. His heart was beating strong as he held her in his arms, watching the sunrise starting to tint the sky. She was sleeping, but all he could do was watch her. He listened to her soft breathing, in awe that this was his wife. The night they'd shared had shown him the way of his heart. He never wanted to let her go. His eyes moved to the bedside table where the journal lay closed. He was thankful for whatever magic brought her here to him.

Rain stirred, opening her eyes. "Good morning." She said as she stretched against him.

"Good morning." Sloan lifted on his elbow, looking down at her with a huge smile. "Did you sleep well?"

"Better than I have in a long time." Rain said, rolling to her side so that she could look at him. "You?"

"I slept great, once I was able to go to sleep." Sloan said, brushing a lock of hair from her cheek.

Rain stretched again, then kissed him. "Won't the men be expecting breakfast?"

"They can starve for all I care." Sloan said, pulling her close.

"I agree." Rain's eyes locked with his.

By the time they went down to get something to eat and some coffee, the sun was bright, and the day had started. Sloan reluctantly left her to go to work, but he gave her a long kiss before he walked out the door. Rain went back upstairs to make up the bed and straighten up. She whistled as she worked. Sloan had told her that he'd be working on the fences today, so he wouldn't be back for lunch. The men were eating at the bunkhouse, so she didn't need to worry about fixing them anything. She had the house to herself.

After she washed off and dressed in her new dress, she walked down to the den to continue reading the book she'd started a couple of days ago. It would be nice to just be lazy for a while. She smiled as she thought about her husband. He'd showed her how much he cared for her and what their life together as a couple would be like. Thoughts of going back to her own time were now forgotten. She'd always have fond memories of her life in New York and her family, but Sloan was her life now.

Rain didn't realize that she'd sat there and read for over three hours until her stomach began to growl. So, she got up and fixed a simple ham and cheese plate. Sloan purchased a large hunk of cheese at the store while she picked out a dress yesterday. She was pleasantly surprised at the flavor in it.

As the afternoon made slow progress into evening, she missed her husband. Rain got up every few minutes to gaze toward the direction Sloan would come from when he returned. She went into the kitchen to stir the pot of soup she'd put together after lunch. A knock at the front door made her smile. He was home.

She rushed to open the door but was let down when it wasn't her handsome husband. A young woman, about her age stood on the other side of the door. "Hello, can I help you?" Rain said, sad it wasn't who she expected.

"Are you Mrs. Weatherby?" The woman asked, her smile too wide to be genuine.

Rain cleared her throat, seeing something in this woman's eyes that told her this was trouble. "I am."

"Then we have a lot to discuss. Can I come in?" The woman said.

"Alright." Rain opened the door and allowed the woman to come inside. "Would you like some lemonade or tea?"

"Lemonade would be nice." The woman said as she sat down in a chair by the fireplace.

"I'll be back in a minute." Rain said, feeling a deep despair wash over her. She just knew something was about to upset her happiness and she couldn't understand why. As a child she'd always been able to see bad things coming, much like her mom. Her heart began to pound in her chest as she walked back into the den carrying a glass of lemonade for her guest. The woman was standing by the shelves, looking at a decorative box that was sitting on a shelf.

"I saw you in the general store yesterday with Sloan. Congratulations on your marriage." The woman said, turning to stare at Rain.

Rain felt a wave of ominous foreboding as the woman's eyes cut into her. She realized this was the woman she'd see that was staring at them. "Thank you." Rain sat up straight and decided to ask this woman what it was that she wanted.

But the woman spoke up first. "I know that you have no idea who I am, but your husband does." The woman said with a harsh tone that told of her agony.

At first Rain just stared at her, then a cold chill ran down her spine. "You're Ruth." Rain stood to her feet, not knowing what to say or do.

Ruth pulled at the lace on her sleeves, "I am."

"But you died with smallpox." Rain was beginning to feel sick. "How can you be sitting here in our den, if you're dead?"

"It's a long story, but I'll get to the point. When I contracted smallpox, my parents had me taken to a hospital that was a long way from here. I was very sick, but somehow through a miracle, I survived. While I was there, I met a doctor and he took care of me. I guess I was a little crazy for a while, so I talked him into telling everyone I died. As far as my parents and Sloan knew, I was dead."

"Why would you do that to your family and Sloan?" Ruth began to get angry.

"The fever had done something to my mind. The moment I got well, I realized that maybe I'd made some bad decisions So, I booked passage back home to make amends and marry the man I love." Ruth said, shrugging her shoulders as though her story was something normal.

"What?" Rain knew something didn't sound right about her story. The hairs on the back of her neck stood straight out with alarm. This woman was crazy.

"You heard me. I know that Sloan will see me and realize that he made a mistake in marrying you." The woman said, trying to look like a victim. "And he loved me long before he became fascinated with you. From what I was told in town, you only showed up here a week or so ago. Sounds like you fool Sloan into marrying you. But I'll make sure that he rights that wrong."

Rain saw through her story. "Sloan won't leave me for you. We've got something wonderful."

"Oh, I'm sure you think so, but when Sloan finds out that I gave birth to his daughter while I was away, he'll change his mind." Ruth said.

Rain's mouth dropped open as she stared at the woman in disbelief. That wasn't something you heard of much in this day. At that moment Sloan walked into the den, his eyes large with surprise.

"Ruth."

Chapter 10

Sloan took a step further into the room, looking from Rain to Ruth. He couldn't believe his eyes. Ruth was dead. "How is this possible?" He wrapped his arms around her, hardly believing what he was seeing.

"Oh Sloan, I've missed you so much. We have a lot to talk about."

Rain wrapped her arms around herself, unable to watch these two have their reunion. When he hears about the child, he'd surely turn away from her and do what was right for his child. But she couldn't just walk out of the room, she had to hear it from him.

Sloan pushed back, still in shock. "Ruth, you were dead. How are you here?"

Ruth told him the same crazy story that she'd told Rain, leaving out the daughter part for a moment. "And here I am." Ruth grasped his hands. "It was hard finding out that you'd married someone else."

"Ruth, you died, or so we were told. I moved on." Sloan said, his eyes going to Rain as she stood with her back to them. He knew she was hurting and confused.

"But now I'm back and we can start over where we left off." Ruth squeezed his hands, drawing his attention back to her.

"That's not possible. I'm married to Rain now." Sloan said, knowing that he planned on staying married to Rain.

Ruth smiled, a strange glint in her eyes. "I have something that will change your mind."

"What's that?" Sloan asked.

"Your daughter." Ruth said in a satisfied tone.

At first Sloan didn't seem to understand her, then he turned his head to look at Ruth. "That's not possible."

"I have proof. She's with my parent right now." Ruth said.

Sloan looked over at Rain again. "Ruth, I think I'd know if it was possible to have a child with you. I'm telling you that's not possible. Ruth, we never had any relations of that nature. So how could I be the father of your child?"

"Don't you remember that night? I never forgot." Ruth purred, putting her hand on his arm.

Sloan took a step backwards. "Ruth, what game are you playing?"

"Sloan, I'm not playing a game. Come to my parent's house and you can see her for yourself. She has your eyes."

Rain put a hand over her mouth as she held back a sob. Could it be true that Sloan and Ruth had a daughter together? She couldn't stand in the way of them making a home for their child. It wouldn't be right. She wouldn't put Sloan through having to make that choice.

Sloan turned away from Ruth and moved toward Rain. When he put his hand on her shoulder, she shrugged it away. "Rain, the child isn't mine. I would know if that was a possibility and it's not. I never... We never... Our relationship wasn't like that."

Rain turned with tears in her eyes. "Sloan, you need to go see for yourself."

"I want you to go with me." Sloan said.

"I'd prefer you didn't bring her around our child." Ruth ground out.

Sloan whirled around. "This is my wife."

"So, you say. Have you found out why she's suddenly here and you're married? Sloan, that's not like you." Ruth's tone was cruel as she looked down her nose at Rain.

"Ruth, I'm happy that you are alive, but that doesn't give you permission to speak of my wife that way." Sloan said. He didn't look toward Ruth but kept his eyes on Rain. "Sweetheart, go with me." He pleaded with Rain.

Rain looked up into his eyes, her heart breaking. "Sloan, this is something you need to do without me. I don't want to do anything to confuse that child."

"But it's not mine." Sloan said again.

A shiver ran down Rain's spine as she looked back at Ruth. "Just go figure it out."

Sloan didn't want to leave Rain here, but he had to get this straightened out. He knew for a fact that this wasn't his child. "I'll only be gone long enough to figure this out."

"Alright." Rain said, then she couldn't resist herself. She pushed up on her toes and kissed him. As their lips touched, she felt a strange feeling run through her. It was as though it would be their last kiss. They looked into each other's eyes for a moment, then he backed away.

"Please, don't go anywhere. I'll be back as soon as I can." Sloan caressed her cheek. "And you know what I mean." He was worried that she'd go back to New York, to the future.

"I'll be here when you get back." Rain said, grasping his arm. She wanted to tell him that she loved him, but she wouldn't do that to him now.

Rain stood in the window and watched him get on his horse to follow Ruth's buggy. Her heart ached as she watched them leave. She believed Sloan, but there was something about Ruth that gave her a dreadful feeling. Something was wrong with her story.

It was late when Rain heard a horse coming down the drive. She ran to the door to greet Sloan. He went past the house, going to the barn to put up the horse. She waited. When he walked in the back door, he looked tired and weary. His eyes met hers and she knew that what he was about to tell her wasn't good.

"Can we sit down?" Sloan said.

"Ok." Rain sat down at the table across from him.

"I don't know how this is possible, but the little girl has my eyes." Sloan looked into her eyes, searching for a response. "I know I never took her to my bed. That's something that I would know."

Rain squeezed her eyes shut. "So, what are you saying, that she's your daughter?"

"It's impossible, but she looks like me. How could that be possible?" Sloan was fighting anger and surprise. When he set eyes on the little girl that was less than two years old, he couldn't help but see the resemblance.

"The only way it's possible is if you are the father. But if you never slept with her, how could she say the child was yours?" Rain was trying to figure this out. Something deep inside of her was setting off warning bells, but she couldn't get her head to wrap around it. She knew he wasn't lying to her because she'd feel it if he was. It was just something she knew. But how did the child look like him? And she was positive that it did because of how pale he was.

"Rain, I'm telling you there's no way that I'm the father. Don't you think I'd remember if I was?" Sloan began to pace back and forth in front of her. "Please say you believe me."

"Sloan, I do believe you. And I also believe that something strange is going on here. For one thing, where has Ruth been for almost two years. And why would she fake her own death?" Rain was trying to think practical and debunk this. Her future depended on it.

Sloan reached out, grasping her hands. "I promise you the child can't be mine. There's one thing that I know for sure and that is I'm an honorable man. If I thought for one minute that it was possible for the little girl to be mine, I'd do the right thing, but I know it's not possible." Then he pulled her into his arms, kissing the top of her head. "We'll figure this out."

Rain sighed as she laid her head against his chest. "Are you hungry? I made soup." She said with a feeling of dread. There was something coming that neither of them could control. But she planned on figuring it out before it destroyed them.

"Sure. Maybe something on my stomach would stop this nausea." Sloan grabbed two bowls as Rain stirred the soup.

"When did the nausea start?" Rain asked, thinking about several reasons he could be nauseous.

Sloan took his bowl of soup and sat down at the table. "As soon as I walked into Ruth's parents' house. It was like something came over me."

That was interesting to Rain. She'd felt something when Ruth was here earlier, but she couldn't explain it just yet. "Did you eat or drink anything while you were there?"

"Just some tea her mother offered me." Sloan stopped his spoon halfway to his mouth. "Rain, her mother wouldn't poison me."

"I'm not so sure about Ruth." Rain said with a raised brow. If only she had her laptop from New York. She could search out this problem.

They ate their soup in silence, both trying to get this into their head. After the dishes were washed, Rain walked to the den where Sloan was staring at the fire. Then her gaze moved to the wooden box that Ruth had been mesmerized with. "Sloan, when Ruth was here, she seemed interested in the wooden box that sits on that shelf."

Sloan turned his gaze toward the shelves, seeing the box. "Oh, that's just a gift she'd given me the week before she came down with smallpox. It's just a box to store tobacco or coins in."

Rain walked over and picked the box up, opening it. There in the box was some sort of potpourri. "What's this inside of it?"

"I think it's dried herbs or something. It did have a scent, but with time it's grown weak."

She placed the box back on the shelf, then turned to her husband. "Let's go up to bed." Rain wanted to comfort her husband and make him know that they were alright.

Sloan's eyes met hers in question. "Let me put another log on the fire, then I'll come up to join you."

Rain changed into her gown, then brushed out her long hair. When she heard Sloan coming up the stairs, she slid between the cool sheets. He walked into their bedroom, his eyes searching out hers. "Are we alright?" He whispered as he set down on the edge of the bed.

"Yes Sloan. Just come to bed." Rain said as she leaned forward and touched his cheek.

Sloan joined her a few minutes later, pulling her into his arms. "I haven't told you, but I was afraid it was too soon. Tonight, I think it's time I confirm my feelings. I love you Rain. Even the first day that I met you, I knew there was something special happening. I fought it for only a moment. Deep inside of me I wanted to make you mine forever."

"There was a definite spark the moment our eyes met when I was in the runaway stage. It was my dream come true. I'm yours, now and forever." Rain lifted her lips to his, letting him know that she felt the same way.

When Sloan pulled her closer, they both knew that together they could weather any storm. That night as they loved one another, time seemed to stop. All they thought about was sharing the magic that seemed to flow between them. Deep into the night, they drifted into sleep with the knowledge that love was what brought them together.

Chapter 11

Rain hummed while she cooked breakfast for the men. Sloan had kissed her before he left for his morning chores. They almost forgot about breakfast, but Sloan pulled back with a grin. "Until tonight my love." Then he'd winked at her, sliding out the door before he changed his mind.

The bacon sizzled in the pan, making the kitchen smell heavenly. Rain pulled the golden biscuits from the oven as the men walked through the back door. She noticed that Sloan wasn't with them. One the of men said that a gentleman had showed up to speak with Sloan, so he was outside still.

A feeling of foreboding filled her as she looked out the kitchen window to see Sloan's face contorted in anger. The man was dressed in a dark suit and held out a few documents toward Sloan, but he pushed them away.

Sloan walked inside a few minutes later, his face still red with anger. "Rain, can we talk?" He looked at her with sad eyes.

Her heart slammed into her ribs as his eyes darted away from hers in pain. She followed him into the den, not wanting to hear what the man in the suit had given him. As she stopped just behind him, Sloan turned and handed the paperwork to her. "It seems Ruth has changed more than I'd thought. She's not giving up on me being the father of her child." He watched her read the legal papers, running his fingers through his hair in frustration.

"Sloan, this says that you knew she was pregnant and helped her fake her death. What is she trying to pull?" Rain's eyes met his. She was furious at this woman that she was beginning to think wasn't who she seemed.

"She's trying to force my hand. I don't know how things are where you're from, but in this day and time, if you father a child and deny it, there can be some consequences. She's basically blackmailing me." Sloan rubbed his forehead, not knowing what to do. This wasn't looking good for him and his ranch.

"So, what can she do to you? Can't you prove that you're not the father?" Rain was having a hard time thinking that it couldn't be proved one way or the other.

"How? It's my word against hers and I'm just a rancher. She's a well-known girl in town. There's the difference. This happened to a friend of mine a couple of years back. He swore it wasn't his kid, but the townsfolks didn't see it that way. He ended up having to marry her even though he hadn't fathered the child. Two years after they married, the real father stepped forward. It was a mess."

"Are you saying that you'll have to marry Ruth? But how can that work since you're married to me?" Rain sat down, her head spinning.

"I won't let you go. This has to be worked out somehow, but I won't divorce you." Sloan took two steps and pulled her into his arms. "Please know that I love you and can't stand the thought of leaving you."

Rain laid her head against his chest as tears of anger and sadness ripped through her. She knew what was about to happen and there was nothing she could do about it. Even though he told her that he couldn't leave her, she knew that in order to keep his ranch and not have to leave town, he'd have to step up. She didn't want to think about that right now. Rain lifted her head and encased his face in her hands.

"I love you Sloan Weatherby and I refuse to let you go, not now or ever. Can we spend the day together? I want to be close to you, please." Then she pushed up, kissing him with a passion she didn't know she had.

Sloan pulled her to him roughly, tasting her tears on her lips. It was his undoing. As he lifted her into his arms, all his thoughts were of her. He carried her up to their bedroom, laying her down on their unmade bed. Their eyes locked as he knelt beside her. "It's just us right now and nobody else. We're together, now." Then he made love to her like he'd never get to again. His tears meshed with hers as they held one another. They loved one another with everything they had.

As they lay together, a storm moved in. Raindrops pounded on the roof and lightning streaked the sky. The thunder rattled the house, but they didn't get up. Sloan pulled her closer, kissing her deeper as the storm roared on outside. He felt as if there was a storm brewing inside their bedroom. Something in her eyes told him that she was saying goodbye. And he couldn't ask her to run away with him, nor could he ask her to stay here and watch him do the right thing even though it wasn't really the right thing.

The storm lasted for over an hour and when it was over, the sun shone through the clouds, streaming across the bed where they lay. Sloan knew that he needed to go check on things at barn after the fierce storm, but he didn't want to let her go. He was afraid of what she'd do when he was gone.

"I need to go check on the men. Stay right here and I'll be back in no time." Sloan said, kissing her forehead before he got up.

"I love you Sloan." Rain said, the tears at the back of her throat almost choking her.

Sloan looked up at her, "Rain, I'll be right back. And I love you more than you can imagine." He leaned down and kissed her lips, then walked out the door.

Rain got up and watched him through the window. Her heart was heavy as she walked back to the bedside table and picked up the journal. He had a decision to make and if she stood in his way, he could lose everything. She couldn't let him do that. The only thing she could think of was to go back to New York and try to forget her cowboy. Deep down she knew that wouldn't be possible. He would be in her heart forever.

She pulled out the page she'd written on to get her here and left it on the dresser for him to find. But at the bottom, she wrote, 'I'll always love you and will never forget you. Yours, Rain'.

Turning to a fresh page in the journal, she picked up her pen and began to write. Her heart ached as she wrote of the love she'd found through the journal. Then as the room began to spin, she heard Sloan yelling for her not to go. She knew that he'd seen her slip through time and out of his life.

When she opened her eyes, she was on her bed. With a sob she lay her head down and began to weep. This wasn't her time. She'd just left the best man and life she could've ever had. But she had to make it easier for him.

With a determination, she stood up and walked into her kitchen. She opened the refrigerator to grab a cold bottle of water. It was as if she'd never left. Then she went to take a long, hot shower. If she was to have any sort of sanity, she'd have to focus on getting her old life back.

The days passed by in slow motion. A month after she came back to New York, she woke with a horrible stomachache. All day she was queasy. After three days of feeling sick, she went to the doctor to see if she had some sort of bug and was surprised to find out that she was pregnant. How could this be? Then she smiled, putting her hand over her abdomen. She was carrying Sloan's baby. His real baby. Tears began to roll down her cheek as his blue eyes filled her thoughts. She missed him so much.

She went to the library to see if she could pull up anything on that time period. If she was lucky, there was something stating whether he married again. Although a lot of records from that time period didn't exist any longer, she took a chance. She didn't find anything, but the librarian told her that maybe the library or county records near where Sloan had lived would tell her more.

So, without hesitation, she booked a flight for the small town outside of Dallas where he'd been. It was a long shot, but she had to know what happened to him. Her first stop after she got her rental car was the library. She went through hours of paperwork but kept coming to a dead end. It was killing her not being able to find anything. Then just as she was about to give up, she found his obituary. Which was odd because there weren't many from that time. But here his was. He'd lived to be eighty-five and was buried in the town cemetery.

She closed out the program and got directions to the old cemetery. It was now a historical site. The library was only a couple of miles from it. With a deep breath, she got out of the car and walked to the old wrought iron fence. She inhaled sharply when she saw the headstones that covered the inside of the fence. How was she going to find him? A breeze began to blow, making her pull her coat tighter around her. She looked up at the clear blue sky with confusion. Why was there an icy breeze? Then as she walked through the gate, a feeling came over her that she wasn't alone.

"Sloan?" Rain whispered, then felt silly. She pulled the journal out of her purse and clutched it. For some reason she felt closer to the him when she had the journal in her hands. "Are you out there somewhere?"

Rain looked around. As she read some of the headstones, she recognized a couple as his workers from the ranch and the owner of the general store was here too. She knew she was in the right cemetery. She walked the rows, reading each headstone. Then as she neared the last row, she saw one with a horse on it. She dropped to her knees in front of the headstone. It was Sloan. Tears formed in her eyes as she saw his name on the headstone. Then the words underneath broke her spirit. 'Husband to Rain, forever searching for her!' She put her hand over her mouth, and her other hand clutched the top edge of the headstone. "Oh Sloan, I'm here my love."

She looked on the right and left of him, but no Ruth. Surely if they'd married, she would be buried beside him. Rain stood up, her mind on finding Ruth in the cemetery, if she was here. As she walked back over the cemetery, she found Ruth's parents, but no Ruth. Then as she started back toward Sloan's headstone, she began to hear a soft voice in her head. Where was it coming from? She looked around, not seeing anyone. For a moment, she stopped walking, hoping the voice would be clearer.

"She's a witch. Go back to him." It came in loud and clear. Rain stood there, unable to believe what she'd just heard on the wind. "What?"

Then as if to answer her, the wind whipped around her like a tornado, engulfing her in a spiral of dust and leaves. At first, she was afraid, then she saw her. Marina was standing in front of her. It was her great, great, grandmother. She'd never seen a picture of her, but she knew what she looked like from the many writings she had of her. "Marina?"

The woman smiled and nodded, "Ruth was a witch. Go back to Sloan and prove it. You know how. It's in your blood. You have the power to take her down and win the man of your dreams. He loves you and is waiting on you." Marina turned and pointed toward Sloan's headstone. "Go to him." Then she was gone.

Rain shook her head. What was happening? She'd never experienced anything like that. It was crazy, but she knew what she had to do. Without hesitation, Rain turned and walked out of the cemetery. She had to remember where Sloan's ranch was from here. Closing her eyes, she imagined when they rode out of town the day she arrived. It was about ten miles out of town to the left. Since the old general store was still here, she knew which way to go.

The ride was slow as she kept looking for places that looked familiar. Then as though it was beckoning to her, there it was. The old house was still standing with the main barn. There had been improvements, but it was Sloan's ranch. The name on the mailbox was Weatherby. Rain gasped as she put her hand on her belly. Was this her great grandchild living here now?

She got out of the car and stood by the fence line. Grabbing a pen, she opened the journal and began to write. As a gust of wind whipped around her, Rain gripped the fence. When she opened her eyes, everything was different. Her heart soared. She just hoped that she was in time.

Chapter 12

Sloan walked out the front door when he heard the wind get up. He'd thought it was a tornado. But then he saw something at the end of the drive. As he looked closer, he saw her, the answer to his prayers. They ran into each other's arms, kissing and hugging. Sloan lifted her and began to spin.

"Sloan, you'll make me throw up." Rain said with a giggle.

"Rain, is it really you?" Sloan said through his tears.

"Yes, my love. It's really me." Rain laid her head against his chest. "And I have news."

Sloan pulled back, "What?"

"I'm pregnant. There's no doubt who the father is." Rain wiped away a tear that slid down her cheek.

At first, he just stared at her, then he shouted. "This is the best news ever." Sloan wrapped his strong arms around her. "Thank you, God."

"Do you remember my ancestor that was the witch?"

"Yes. The one that put the spell on the journal, right?"

"That's the one. She came to me and told me to come back to you. Marina said that Ruth is a witch. She told me to expose her for what she is, and all will be well."

"And how do we do that?" Sloan said, not sure about that.

"I don't know." Rain laughed. She was happy being back in Sloan's arms to care. "What's happened in my absence?"

"Well, I've managed to get a reprieve from Ruth's lawyer. He said that they will have a special chemist come in from somewhere up north that can analyze my blood against the child's. It could take a month or so to get them here."

"At least we have time to figure out how to prove what she is. If I've got this right, she's done something to make the child look like you." Rain kissed his cheek. "I've missed you."

"Oh, you have no idea. It's been horrible here without you." Sloan put his arm around her as they walked back to the house. "When I walked into the room as you disappeared, my world stopped. I almost lost my mind for a moment, but something told me that you'd be back."

They walked into the house and Rain looked around at the familiar surroundings. "This place is still standing in 2020. Can you believe it? I saw it and that's where I wrote in the journal to come back to you."

Sloan smiled, "I'm not surprised. This place is built well." Then he looked down at her.

"Are you happy about the baby?" Rain asked, unsure if it was too soon in their life together. It has been a whirlwind relationship and now a baby.

"Beyond happy. This is the best news I could've heard." Sloan turned as the back door opened and the men started in for dinner. "Guys, she's back. I told you she'd be back. And we're having a baby." Sloan blurted it all out at once, making the men laugh. They congratulated them, slapping him on the back and giving her hugs. That evening Sloan and Rain celebrated their news with the men. Rain was glad she'd came back home. And that's what this was, her home.

Sloan went out to get more wood for the fire while Rain finished washing up the dishes. He dropped a kiss on the back of her neck when he passed by on his way to the den. "I missed you."

Rain walked in the room to join him by the fire. "I missed sitting by the fire at night." She said as she settled into the chair that was situated by the hearth.

"Is that all you missed?" Sloan said in a low voice, his eyes on her. He couldn't believe she was back here with him. He'd prayed every night for her return and here she was.

"No, it isn't." Rain leaned forward, reaching for his hand. "I missed you something fierce."

"Can I ask why you decided to go back when you did? I know things were crazy, but we were just starting our life together." Sloan asked as he knelt in front of her, wanting to be near her.

Rain was quiet for a moment, wanting to word her answer as best she could. "I knew that for you to make the best decision for you, I had to be out of the picture. If I was here, you'd choose me, and I didn't want you to feel pressured. Maybe it wasn't the best choice, but I did make a decision about our future while I was there."

Sloan sat back, not sure if he wanted to hear what she decided. "And what was that?"

"I decided that being with you here was better than all of the things I thought I missed when I was in the future." Rain giggled. "I even caught myself not turning on lights as I went into rooms. I lit candles and sat in the soft light of its glow, missing you."

"Can we start over then? I want to make you the happiest woman on earth." Sloan pushed forward on his knees, reaching up to touch her face. "I don't have much to offer other than this ranch and my love, but it's yours. I'm yours, forever." His eyes sought hers.

Tears formed in Rain's eyes as she looked deep into his eyes. "And I'm yours forever. I don't need anything but you, my love."

Sloan leaned forward, touching his lips to hers as he grasped her arms, pulling her toward him.

He'd dreamed of holding her like this while she was gone. Some nights he'd wake up and look at her side of the bed, missing her warmth. Now she was here with him. He couldn't get close enough to her. He'd missed her and just the thought of having her back here was almost too much. His heart was aching from the pleasure of seeing her and knowing they'd have a baby as proof of the love they shared.

When Sloan stood to his feet, he brought her up with him. Then he turned and sat down in the chair, pulling her down onto his lap. His large, strong arms wrapped around her as she lay her head against his shoulder. They sat like that for a long while, just enjoying being together again. He'd never let her go again. If it took his last breath, he'd make sure she always wanted to be right here with him. She was his life and the life she carried within her was his future. He closed his eyes as he lay his hand over her abdomen. The life there was their legacy.

"Let's go to bed. I'm tired." Rain said as she yawned.

Sloan frowned, "Is everything alright with the baby?"

Rain kissed his chin, "Yes, our baby is just fine." Then she thought about the purse she had with her when she came this time. It held a gift for her husband. "I'll go up and change into my gown. I have a gift for you."

She went upstairs and changed, noticing he'd left her clothes in the drawer as they had been when she left. A small smile crossed her lips as she slid in between the sheets with his surprise in her hand. She heard him coming up the stairs. Her heart skipped a beat when he came through the door. Would just the sight of him always make her heart do that? Somewhere in her mind, she knew it would.

After he changed and climbed into bed beside her, Rain handed him the sonogram photo. Then she held the lamp close for him to get a better look. "I know it's not a lot to see, but this is our baby." She pointed to the blip at the bottom of the picture.

Sloan gave her a strange look, then pulled the picture closer. "How is this possible?"

"They have an imaging camera that they run over my stomach. It can take pictures of the baby in my womb. They can measure him or her that way and look to see if everything is alright. He or she is not much bigger than a plumb right now, but everything is fine. The doctor gave me a clean bill of health just a couple of days ago."

He couldn't stop looking at the sonogram. "So, this is our baby?" Sloan turned to look at her, tears welling in his eyes. "Thank you for this. I'm amazed and in love with our unborn child already."

"And I'm in love with the daddy." Rain whispered as she felt her heart melt at the way he looked at their unborn child. She turned and placed the lamp back on the bedside table, turning the wick down. When she turned back around, Sloan pulled her into his embrace, kissing the top of her head.

"I've spent so many nights wanting you right here in my arms. Thank you for coming back." Sloan kissed his way down her face until he reached her lips, then he pulled back slightly. "Never leave me again." His voice was husky with emotion.

"Never." Rain reached up to touch his face, memorizing every detail. "Tomorrow we will figure the mess with Ruth out, but tonight is for reuniting and renewing our love."

Sloan crushed his lips to hers, their love taking over as they found what they'd been missing. Both forgot about anything other than each other as the moon made its slow trip across the night sky.

Chapter 13

For two days Rain spent her time writing down everything she could remember from the books she'd read on witchcraft. She knew that if only there was a library close by, she could do this in a shorter time. The evening of the second day, Sloan sat down at the table beside her, giving her a cup of coffee as he turned the wick up to make the lamp brighter.

"Any luck?"

"Let me ask you something, when Ruth came here the first time to tell you about the child, did she seem different?" Rain asked. She'd been trying to figure out when things changed for Ruth.

Sloan thought for a minute, "Actually, Ruth had always been so kind and sweet. She never liked conflict. It surprised me when her whole demeanor was about causing conflict when she was here."

"Did you notice any of that before she got sick?"

"No." Sloan raised a brow. "Do you think something happened while she was away at the hospital?"

"Seems likely." Rain tapped her pencil on the paper, then gasped. "Where was the hospital?"

Sloan shrugged, "It was somewhere in Louisiana called New Orleans."

Rain's eyes grew large with surprise. "That's it. She must have met a witch there. New Orleans has a side to it that could have affected her. We need to figure this out. I want to talk to Ruth."

"That won't happen, I won't let it. If she is a witch or bewitched, I don't want anything happening to you or our unborn child." Sloan reached out to place his hand over her abdomen. "I'll protect both of you with my life."

"I can protect myself." Rain said. "My mother taught me and my sisters how to do some things. Even though we didn't practice witchcraft, we had some knowledge of spells."

"NO, I won't let you take that chance." Sloan grasped her hand. "There has to be another way."

"Ok, I'll see if I can figure it out." Rain knew that the only way to see if Ruth was bewitched was to look at her. She'd have to figure out a way to see her without Sloan getting suspicious.

"What are you thinking?" Sloan said as he looked her expression.

"Nothing." Rain said.

"Don't do anything stupid." Sloan wrapped his arm around her, "If I have to tie you to me, I will."

Rain giggled, "You won't have to resort to that."

"Good to hear."

While Sloan put extra logs on the fire, Rain went up to change for bed. Her mind was on the need to figure this out. Then without warning, a voice came out of nowhere. "Rain, it's a spell she's under. She carries a sachet that holds a spell."

Rain stood still for a moment, knowing it was Marina. "But how do I get it from her?"

"You'll find the way in the journal." Marina said in a wispy voice.

Rain looked up just as the voice disappeared. She jumped when Sloan spoke from just behind her. "Darling, who are you talking to?"

"Oh, just myself." Rain waved her hand to dismiss it.

"You were having a full-on conversation with yourself?" Sloan gave her a strange look as he pulled his suspenders down his arms.

Rain laughed, "I tend to do that from time to time. Just overlook my quirkiness." She knew that it would be too much on him to tell of Marina's visit. Maybe one day she'd tell him more about her ancestor, but for now, that would be her secret. "Let's get some sleep."

"I'll be getting an early start to town in the morning. Is there anything you need while I'm there?" Sloan asked as he changed for bed.

"I want to go with you." Rain knew this would be the opportunity she needed.

"That's not a good idea. I don't want you getting upset if we run into Ruth." Sloan shook his head.

Rain walked over and touched his arm, "But Sloan, I want to go. I won't get upset if I see her. Please, let me go."

Sloan rolled his eyes, "Woman, you will be the death of me. I just know it. Fine, since I can't seem to say no to you, then you can go."

"Thank you." Rain pushed up on her toes to kiss him. "Now, let's get some sleep."

The next morning, they left for town just as the sun was beginning to rise in the sky. The air was chilly, but Rain was wrapped in a blanket that Sloan had insisted on bringing. Only a mile or so into the ride and she was glad to have the blanket. They talked about the baby, the list of supplies needed at the store and the fog that seemed to come in suddenly.

When they arrived in town, things seemed quiet. There was nobody on the street and the fog seemed to engulf the town from one end to the other. "This fog is crazy." Sloan said as he helped her down from the wagon seat.

Rain just looked around, expecting to see something coming out of the fog at the end of the street at any moment. "Yes, it is." She mumbled, knowing it wasn't a coincidence that the fog was surrounding the town.

The store owner greeted them when they walked through the door. "Good morning Sloan, Mrs. Weatherby." The man said, taking the list that Sloan gave him. "I'll be glad when this fog lifts. Is it foggy out your way Sloan?"

"No, not at all. When did it roll in?" Sloan asked, looking back to make sure Rain was still close by. There was something ominous about the morning that had Sloan feeling a little off.

"Yesterday. It was the strangest thing and as you can see from the empty streets, it has everyone staying inside. I'm glad to see you both out and about." The gentleman said, then he looked at Rain. "And I'm glad to see you are back from your trip."

At first Rain stared at the man, then her eyes met Sloan's. "OH, yes, thank you. I'm glad to be back."

Sloan smiled warmly as he touched her cheek. "And she came back with news of the upcoming birth of our first child."

The store owner clapped his hands together. "That is exciting news. Congratulations to you both."

"Thank you." Sloan said. "Rain, is there anything you need while we're in town?"

"I'll look around and see." Rain said, her eyes on the door. She could feel something coming and it wasn't more fog. In her mind she knew it was the cause of the fog that was about to walk through the door. Her eyes darted from Sloan to the door. She wasn't too sure how this would go down, but Sloan's safety was one of her priorities as well as her unborn child.

The bell over the door alerted her that Ruth was here. It was apparent that she wasn't alone. She was pushing a carriage. Her smile broadened when she saw Sloan, but then she flinched. Her head pivoting to the right as she felt Rain's presence. The two women's eyes met in a fierce inward battle of wills. Ruth pulled her gaze from Rain, turning her attention on Sloan.

"Sloan, my darling. I'm so glad to see you." Ruth purred, pushing the carriage over to his side. "Your daughter and I were just out for a beautiful morning stroll."

Sloan went still as he heard Ruth's voice. His gaze found Rain's and she nodded. Their plan was for Sloan to get Ruth occupied, then Rain would figure out where the talisman was that was causing the spell. According to Marina, it was something ordinary, but only Rain would sense it. As Rain took a step toward the woman, she felt a breeze beside her. "I'm right here with you my child." Rain breathed a sigh of relief as she realized that her long lost great, great grandmother was here to see this through. "She's after you and your unborn child. The child you carry has a strong power that she wants to harness."

Rain nodded and took another step. She watched Ruth as she touched Sloan's arm, laughing at something he said. Sloan's face was rock hard as he tried to keep the conversation going. "What a beautiful little girl." Rain said, looking into the carriage. The child did look like Sloan.

Ruth whirled around, looking uncomfortable as Rain moved around the carriage, her eyes on Ruth. "What are you doing? Stay away from my child."

Sloan held up his hand, "Rain means no harm to your child. She's just looking at her." Sloan said between his clenched teeth. "Ruth, you can be one of the first to hear the news. Rain and I are expecting a child."

Ruth began to turn red with anger. Rain saw it as an opportunity to figure out the placement of the spell. "Yes, Ruth, we are expecting a child. And this one is in fact, Sloan's." Rain's eyes bore into Ruth's and they stood glaring at one another.

"Are you saying my daughter is not his also? What kind of trickery is this?" Ruth spat out.

"No, what kind of trickery is this?" Rain pointed toward the child in the carriage, then back at Ruth. "When you went away after you got sick with smallpox, were you visited by a woman?"

Ruth was too angry at first to answer her, then something changed. "So, you know who I am?"

The voice with which Ruth spoke wasn't hers. It was that of a deranged old woman. Rain looked up at Sloan and nodded. The fact that Marina was so close had brought out the spell itself. Ruth seemed confused by what she'd said, but Rain put her hand on the woman's arm and squeezed it. "I'm quite aware of who you are and I'm sure you know who's beside me." Rain said with a slight smile.

The woman began to shake, but Rain didn't let go of her. Even Sloan began to see the shaking. He was afraid for Rain, but she held up her other hand and motioned for him to stay back. Marina was speaking now, her tone too low for even Rain to hear. But the spell inside of Ruth was listening.

As the spell grew stronger, ready for attack, so did Marina.

When Rain felt movement to her side, she looked around and the most beautiful woman was standing beside her. She knew in an instant that it was Marina. Marina's focus was on Ruth, but one of her hands was on Rain's shoulder. Rain heard Sloan's sharp intake of breath as he also saw Marina appear.

"What?" Sloan said. He looked around and saw that the shop owner was going about his business as though none of this was happening.

Marina smiled at Sloan and nodded. Then she focused on Ruth. "Be gone, you're not welcome here in this place."

Rain seemed to pale a little as she continued to hold onto Ruth's arm. When Sloan noticed it, he started toward her, but Marina held out her hand for him to take it. At first, he wasn't sure, then something in her eyes gave him the strength. "Trust me."

Ruth began to collapse, but Sloan caught her just as her legs buckled. He carried her to the chair beside the wood stove in the center of the store. "Ruth, are you alright?" He said as her eyes fluttered open.

"Sloan, I'm so sorry for all of this. I couldn't control anything going on. Please forgive me." Ruth began to cry as she looked toward Rain. She didn't see Marina. "Thank you."

"You'll be fine now." Rain repeated Marina's whispered words. Then Rain looked down at the little girl in the carriage. She no longer looked like Sloan. She was still a beautiful child, but the spell was gone.

"I married the doctor that helped me when I was sick. She's his. He will be looking for us. When the old woman gave me the herbs to help with the pain after the baby was born, that's when everything went crazy."

Rain began to feel weak as she leaned against the counter. Sloan was by her side before she could think. "Darling, are you alright?"

Marina smiled as she placed her hand over Rain's womb. "She's alright and your son is doing just fine."

Sloan looked up at Marina, tears filling his eyes. "My son?"

"Oh yes, you have a son coming. And he's healthy as is his mother." Marina touched Rain's cheek, "I'll be seeing you again one day."

"Marina, if you see my parents, please tell them I love them." Rain said.

"I will."

Then Marina vanished in a mist, leaving them.

"Let's go home." Sloan said as he paid the unknowing store owner.

Chapter 14

On their way home, Sloan turned to Rain. "Are you planning to tell me what I just witnessed in the store?"

Rain giggled, touching her stomach. "Well, Marina has figured out her time travel skills. She got wind that something evil was going on around me and evidently this witch wanted revenge on Marina through me."

"So, she just moves around from time to time?"

"I guess. I've never really talked to her before." Rain shrugged. "All I can say is, it's kind of like having a fairy godmother. And I'm glad she showed up when she did because I don't know what was about to happen."

"Do you really think she knew what our baby is?" Sloan rasped, still reeling from everything he'd seen.

"I'm pretty sure she does." Rain wrapped her arm around his and laid her head against his upper arm. "Are you happy it's a boy?"

"As long as he or she is healthy, I don't care. And of course, you are healthy too." Sloan smiled, clicking his tongue to put the horses in a faster stride. "Let's get back home my love. We have some catching up to do."

Rain giggled, feeling a warmth spread over her. The love she had for Sloan was unmeasurable and to think that they would soon have a son made her want to scream it to the world.

With each passing day, Rain showed more and more. Through everything that they'd gone through, their love had endured. Rain learned how to cook biscuits without catching the oven on fire and Sloan learned how to have patience with his pregnant wife.

One day when she was almost eight months along, Sloan came in with a surprise. He'd found a puppy on the ride back from town. "I thought you'd love to have him to grow up with our son." Sloan said as he put the puppy in her hands.

"Oh Sloan, he's precious." Rain held the puppy close, kissing the top of his soft head. "What shall we call him?"

"I don't know. It's your dog." Sloan pointed out as he washed his hands before dinner.

"I'll call him Granger for my maiden name."

"Good choice." Sloan rubbed the puppies head. "I'll find him a box to put in the corner of the den."

The men came in, acting like children when they saw the puppy. Rain laughed at the way they crouched on the floor, playing with Granger. She imagined them with the baby. Their baby would be showered with love in this house.

When the men left to go back to the bunkhouse, Rain sat watching the puppy sniffing up at the table. "I'll find him something to put a little food and water in. I'm sure he's hungry." Rain said in a childlike voice as she gave the puppy another pat on the head.

Sloan rolled his eyes, "You would understand that." Then he slipped out the door before she could react.

Rain found two small empty butter tins from butter in the cellar, so she scrambled the little puppy an egg and gave him water. After he was fed, she turned to finish the dishes.

The feeling of dread washed over her as she placed the last dish in the cupboard. What was it? She looked around for a sign that something was wrong, but everything looked fine. Then as she shrugged, thinking it was just in her mind, a sharp pain ran through her abdomen. When she cried out, the puppy was by her side, barking.

Sloan was on his way back to the house with the crate he'd found when he heard the puppies frantic barking. He broke into a run. Rain was on the floor, clutching her stomach as she cried out in pain. He didn't know what to do. "Rain, what's wrong?"

"I don't know. Maybe the baby is coming early." Rain said as another pain ripped through her.

"The baby. No, no, no." Sloan waved his hands around. "It's not time, right. What do we do?"

"I've never had a baby, so I have no clue." Rain said, looking up at her husband's frantic face. "You've helped with the birth of cows and horses, haven't you?"

Sloan looked at her strangely, then began to laugh. "I don't think it's the same darling. I'll run tell one of the guys to get the doctor after I get you to the bed."

"Ok." Rain whispered as fear ran through her. She didn't know what to do and here she was in a time without epidurals. What was she thinking? Then she looked at her husband's handsome face and she knew what she was doing. "Tell them to hurry because your son is getting a little anxious to make an exit."

"Well, tell him to slow down." Sloan said as he rushed out the door after he made sure she was settled onto the bed. When he returned, one of the older men was with him. "Jacob helped his wife with the birth of their son, so he came to stay with us until the doctor gets here."

Rain smiled at Jacob. "Thanks." Then she grabbed her belly again.

"We need hot water, and extra sheet and some whiskey." Jacob said, looking a little out of sorts as he watched Rain gasp in pain.

"What's the whiskey for?" Sloan asked.

Jacob laughed as he walked out, headed for the stairs. "For you my friend. You'll need it, believe me."

A couple of hours later, Sloan knew why Jacob brought the whiskey and a glass to him. It was horrible watching his wife in pain and knowing that there was nothing he could do. Jacob had been great. He knew what to get ready in the case that the doctor didn't arrive on time. Sloan just prayed that he did because he wasn't sure that he was ready to deliver his son by himself. What if something went wrong? He couldn't lose Rain, not after all they'd gone through to get to this point.

Rain grasped his hand, bringing him out of his daydream. "Sloan..." She was trying to speak in between the pain. "I think we're about to meet our son."

"Not yet darling. The doctor should be here soon." Sloan sat beside her, wiping her brow as she cried out again. Deep down he knew that their son was coming without the doctor. Jacob had walked him through what needed to be done when the time came. He'd be there to help, but Sloan would be the one delivering his son.

Jacob rushed into the room when she cried out. "The pains are getting closer Sloan. It's almost time. I've got water boiling to disinfect the items you'll need." Then Jacob looked at Rain. "I'll be at your head, but Sloan will be in charge. That's if it's alright with you."

Rain nodded her head, "I'm ok with that." She knew he was the only one in the room that knew what to do.

The baby was ready, and Sloan got in position to bring his son into the world. He was nervous, but with the help of Jacob, he knew they'd have a baby soon. "Alright darling, I see the top of his head."

Jacob grasped Rain's shoulders. "Now, it's all up to you Rain."

Rain's body took over as the natural birthing process began as it had for centuries upon centuries.

Rain let out a loud yell as their son entered the world. Sloan grasped him in a clean sheet and did as Jacob told him. Once the baby cried, Sloan and Rain looked at one another and laughed. Their son had a good set of lungs alright. Just as Sloan placed their son in Rain's arms, the doctor came through the door.

"Sloan, Rain, looks like I'm a few minutes late." The doctor said as he checked on Rain, then looked up at the couple. "Sloan, you did good. And you have a healthy son. What's his name?"

Sloan gave Rain a small smile. "We've decided that the baby will be named Phillip Silas Weatherby after both our fathers."

"Good solid name." The doctor said as he went out to wash his hands.

Once Jacob and the doctor left, Sloan sat down on the edge of the bed, putting his arm around Rain's shoulders. "He's perfect."

"Just like his father." Rain said, lifting her head to kiss her husband.

"Have I told you lately that I'm glad you chose me?" Sloan said, then he kissed the top of his son's head.

"Not in the last couple of hours, but I never grow tired of hearing it." Rain looked down at their son's sleeping face. "I love you Sloan Weatherby and I can't imagine life without you."

"Love doesn't even describe how I feel about you. I can't breathe without thinking about you. And you've just made me happier than I thought I could ever be." Sloan whispered as tears choked him.

Rain let the tears slip down her cheeks as she looked back up at her husband. "It's crazy that this time last year I was sitting in a board room, discussing the newest authors coming down the pike. And now, I'm sitting here with my husband, holding our son. I'm overwhelmed with love. Thank you."

"No, thank you." Sloan kissed her lips.

Their life was filled with more love than either could imagine. The next summer, they had a daughter and named her Marina Faith. Sloan said it was only fitting that their daughter be named after the woman that made it possible for them to find one another. Together they'd found more than love, they'd found forever...

Rain knew that through Marina's spell, she'd found the Cowboy of Her Dreams...

If you love incredible journeys, then The Pirate of Her Desire, book 3 in The Journal series, will give you the journey of a lifetime.

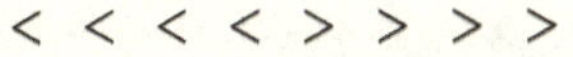

And now, here's a look at To Dance with

Dragonflies…

Chapter 1

The sun was coming over the horizon when Kaity raced down the steps of her house. She couldn't be late again. Mr. Harris was already upset with her. She turned the key in the ignition, but nothing happened. Great, just great. The battery had finally given up the fight. She'd saved for a new battery, but then she blew a tire three days ago and had to use that money to buy a tire. Why was God testing her? Then she said a prayer asking for forgiveness because she questioned Him.

With a groan, she got out of the car and grabbed her bag. She'd have to run to catch the bus at the end of the block. Even as she started up the sidewalk the bus was coming to a stop. Waving her hands frantically as she ran, trying to catch the attention of the driver. Then just as she reached the back corner of the bus, it pulled away from the curb.

Kaity let out a long sigh. "This isn't going to be my day." Then she looked up toward the sky. "I know, I know. There's a reason that I missed the bus and my car wouldn't crank. So, when are you planning to let me in on this great plan you have for me?" She giggled as a man walking down the sidewalk gave her a crazy look. "And now I look like I've lost my mind."

Just as she turned to start the three mile walk to work, she stumbled, loosing grip on her purse. As the contents spilled onto the sidewalk, Kaity cried out. She rushed to grab everything. Once she had her stuff back in the purse, she stood up, stumbling again, but a hand grasped her elbow, startling her.

"Are you alright?" The masculine voice came from the most beautiful man she'd ever set eyes on.

At first, she couldn't speak. She only managed to mutter something unintelligible as she looked into the blue eyes that were looking at her in concern. Her mouth opened, but nothing came out. When she regained her senses, she spoke. "I'm fine, just clumsy." Kaity frowned as he let go of her elbow.

"I saw you running for the bus, do you need a ride somewhere?" The gorgeous man asked as she continued to stare at him.

"Oh... I... well... yes. But I don't know you." Kaity responded.

The man stuck out his hand, "I'm Derek Mason. And yourself?"

"Oh, me?" Kaity bit her lower lip, a bought of shyness sweeping over her. "My name is Kaity, Kaity Johnson."

"Well, Kaity Johnson, it looks like we're no longer strangers. Now, let me drive you to where you need to go." Derek said. He'd been seeing her here and there since he'd moved to town. She intrigued him with her shy smile that seemed to light up a room. Then when he'd seen her running up the sidewalk, waving for the bus, he'd stopped to watch her.

"It seems so. But I can't trouble you." Kaity began to shake her head.

"Where are you headed? It's no trouble or I wouldn't have offered." Derek knew she was different from any woman he'd ever known. The green of her eyes seemed to pull him in and make him want to find out why there was ever any sadness in their depths. She looked up at him and he was lost.

"Work." Kaity said, not realizing that he had no idea where that was.

"And where is that?" Derek said with a grin.

"Aroma Coffee at the corner of Elm and Grey streets." Kaity looked at her phone and knew she'd be late in five minutes.

"I know the one." Derek led her to the sports car parked just up the street. "And I'll get you there before nine."

I hope you enjoyed this small look into the sweet, Christian romance, To Dance with Dragonflies. It's available at most online retailers!

About the Author

Stephanie Hurt was born in Georgia. She currently lives in Pike County, Georgia, along with her husband Tommy and son Hunter. Along with writing, she's an accountant and children's minister. She has been writing stories since she was a teenager, but only in the last couple of years decided to publish her novels. She mainly writes romance novels.

Stephanie Payne Hurt loves to hear from fans!

Connect with Author:

Twitter: https://twitter.com/StephanieHurt4

Email: https://stephaniehurt4@gmail.com

Website: www.stephaniehurtauthor.com

Facebook:

https://www.facebook.com/StephaniePayneHurt

Sign up for my newsletter at

www.stephaniehurtauthor.com to keep up with

upcoming events and new releases.

<u>Please give a review and let her know</u>

<u>what you thought!</u>